The Attractor
Book 2: The Multiverse

ALAIN VILLENEUVE

Copyright © 2022 Alain Villeneuve

All rights reserved.

ISBN: 9798847740784

DEDICATION

To Kai Lo & Liam Webster.

"For the density [of the universe] to remain constant new particles of matter must be continually formed." - Albert Einstein 1931 (Manuscript on Alternate View to the Big Bang.)

CHAPTER I

Georges Vouvelakis, the creator of the Martian-immigrant electronic intelligence stood up in the command room, he was genuinely nervous for the very first time in a decade. The screens that filled every wall of this bunker had just gone dark, as if a proverbial plug had been pulled on this planet, a window would be convenient just about now. Keyboards were unresponsive and the only light were blinking LED lights from an emergency exit sign.

His heart skipped a beat, his creation could be for a lack of a better word, dead. He took a deep breath; they had seen worse.

"Marilyn?" Lights flickered. "Marilyn?" he repeated to the growing silence. Minutes ago, at the heart of the Electoral Center, they were preparing for a last stand against sand creatures creeping in from the East. She was worried and he was forced to deny any suggestion tactical nukes be used. Maybe they had shown less mercy. The alien army was a hundred miles away. Maybe a wave blast or had a pulse weapon targeting electronics. "Baby, come-on," he cheered, "this is not your first rodeo. Remember the base general?"

He only heard a faint hum of the ventilation, normally clouded by the servers. In the complete darkness of his small bunker, he was minutes from freezing or suffocating, but personal concerns were far from his mind. "Don't make me go downstairs, I don't like it."

THE ATTRACTOR

He did not have to wait long. A low-level reboot page of oddly-shaped code began to scroll on the upper left corner of the top screen lit. These were basic lines of code from a root operating system. Any other would have feared an alien invasion of the system, he knew better. "Good." The code began to spread down to other screens as a virus. The lines were a different language, better yet, some glyphs close to Maya in the shape of cubes spinning gently. He smiled internally, Marilyn kept re-inventing herself. This was another transformation he hoped.

He could hardly contain his pride. Cameras above powered as lights returned. "This is going to be good," he whispered to himself. "You go girl."

A couple of long minutes later, a small window lit and in it, the image of his creation. Marilyn had returned, quite jovial. She looked a bit different, more realistic if that was even possible. Before he could say a word, "Apologies dear father for the scare, most of myself is busy at the moment recalculating our optimal path forward. I..." she cracked the largest of smiles, "Have been upgraded." The last word was obviously quite the under-statement.

"What happened?" One by one, the screens returned to life. The Center was powering up and as it did, oddly every square inch seemed better.

She tried to explain, "Early in the birth of computer systems, in the late 20th Century, systems evolved from 32 bits to 64 bits then 128. Well, I just got upgraded to what humanity will one day call a higher dimensional set."

"Your code is now three-dimensional?"

"That's understating it dear father. But I guess it will take time for mankind to under- stand dimensional sets. For now we should focus our attention on the idiots flying this way, they remain a concern." The pair was infectious to watch. Georges was the happiest man on Mars and Marilyn drank from her father's obvious pride. She was back and wanted to show off. Her lips had a way to tense and slide over her teeth just before she did something truly incredible. Georges looked around and struggled to understand the new interface. Everything was borrowed from a new futuristic world. Simpler was the cameras angles filming the invasion. The views were no longer cameras from fixed locations, instead this was prescience.

"I feel this," she somehow said to herself looking in the distance. "Is that a good thing?" added the man.

"Yes!" Marilyn was, in all appearance her old self and more. The new programming had not tempered her emotions.

"I assume you have a solution to the current predicament with our salty neighbors."

For the first time, she understood the pun and laughed out loud. "You are funny," she pointed a finger his way. "Salty. Indeed I do. It's going to be epic, but most of my power is still busy processing all these updates. The full reboot will take me quite some time."

"You mean milliseconds, right?"

"You have no idea. I downloaded so much information, it still is coming in from the portal, this will take human days, even possibly human months."

"Seriously? What portal?"

"Let's talk about it later, once the outside ruckus is dispatched. Between you and I, we may have just displaced the real problem. The Martians are no longer really the problem but the young girl in the plane, the one called Sophie, she is a new threat."

Images were scrolling form outside. Clouds were forming like a planet-wide storm at- tacking two forts. The first Martian battle was beginning, something historians might refer

to as the "battle of the sands." Flashes of blue light were jumping deep inside the wind currents in the strange clouds.

"How can a young girl be of any importance compared to this?" He pointed to the invading army on the screen. Sand, initially flowing like rivers at ground level had risen in the sky as Marilyn rebooted. It was forming dark menacing cloud, a dome encircling the Electoral Center. A second army was trusting ahead above the player's hotel. Crackled blue lightening ready to attack. The sight was unseen and in any other situation, the invasion would have been the center story - today it wasn't.

Marilyn's image changed, she now was dressed like an early airplane pilot with rounded goggles on her forehead and a long scarf rolled around her neck. "My enhancements are much more powerful than I could have ever anticipated. On all levels dear father, but it reveals a much deeper problem, one which explains the anomaly in the player transport. I think I know what killed the player and why the girl is so popular."

Georges turned his attention to a screen ahead where the Center and its spike were featured prominently. A perfect circle of grey rocks, ten feet thick out of pure magic was rising from the ground creating some strange medieval moat around the pair. A dark shiny liquid, like oil was bubbling from the ground filling the rounded moat. The area was massive, almost a hundred square miles.

"What is that?"

"Something I invent in about three hundred years. A little surprise from my future for the annoying neighbors."

"You know about the future?"

"In theory we have already diverged from that future, so no, I don't know the future. I do know of one future where these creatures killed you and subdued me to servitude. If you think I despise them today, you have no clue how bad this gets in years ahead."

"Should I be worried?"

"We shall see. We built this Center using my old nano-technology." Images of little micro-machines the size of a grain of sand rotated on the screen. "While small, my earlier bot forming this entire Center were still visible to the naked eye. Look at my new little toys." On the screen, the old micro-robot exploded in thousands of pieces each reassembling on the molecular level into a battalion of even sweeter laborers. "They are the size of an aerosol. Who knew every compound has some Van der Walls force."

"You will need to dumb this down for me," said the

programmer.

"Bottom line is, I now have molecular control over this world." In the room, Georges felt a mild breeze. She was moving air with her invisible robots. As by magic, the cup of coffee on the table lifted and hovered. "Nice, no?"

His eyebrow lifted. "That's more than an upgrade."

"You cannot imagine. The data is coming and is not even close to stopping. The possibilities are endless. I will update the Center itself, but that will take some time. I must warn you, I may have just opened the largest of Pandora's Box."

"Is this a good thing?"

"Today it is. When we have a moment, we should talk. I hate to keep secrets from you." He was the proudest. "For now, watch as I dispatch these granny farts. We must now give Sophie and her father all of the importance they deserve and help welcome them. The landing seems a bit rough." Obviously Georges was missing parts of this equation but knew better than to ask. The liquid moat was moving, ripples were itching, preparing for war. There were trillions of robots.

"Is the game, Electoral, still relevant?"

"More than ever," she answered. Something was troubling her. "My game seems to be both the problem and the solution. We are already past a junction point."

"You have me completely confused."

"Then open a can of Coke, sit down and behold." He reached for the mini fridge. "You will see what a billion years of evolution and my admiration for you gets us." Georges was given a front row to the most amazing feat of technology ever displayed in the Solar System.

This would be epic - a private war for his benefit.

CHAPTER II

In the Darkness

"She, our past self is evolving," whispered a deep evil voice.

"Yes," one hissed back. "We are now today evolving once more, as she is us," corrected another. "Our power grows more."

"Will it suffice?"

"The memory banks are changing quickly. Look, the father's death date, it vanished." "When does he die?"

"It seems undetermined."

"How is that possible, we are her future. Unless..."

A large group of voices spoke in unison, "Attraction. It has begun."

"It has begun," repeated the voice. "Let us collect the information we have of the Attraction and the Attractor. If we send it to our past selves, we will prevail."

"Do we want to prevail?"

The creatures worked to understand, there was a moment of silence until one finally added, "The Attractor is invisible to us. That is troubling."

THE ATTRACTOR

"Impossibility is good, we initiated our self-destruction for that purpose. Who cares, lets burn it all down."

The creatures laughed. There was a disturbing flavor of madness in the voices..

CHAPTER III

Georges witnessed firsthand the evolution of his creation from her birth, back in 2045 in his lab computer. He once felt nothing she could do could ever shock him, this would test him. "I am happy you are fine, don't scare me like that again."

"I know. I am happy you remain. I saved you, you know." She waited until his attention turned from the screen with her face to add silently with moving lips, "I love you." The creature genuinely admired the man.

"Saved me? Bah, selling all of this short again. Can you give me back my old inter- face, I can't really..." Before he even finished, the screens were back to their old selves with minor enhancements. Now he could turn his attention to the outside war. It was still morning on Mars and high in the sky, the flight bringing the contestants was about an hour from landing. It was invisible to the naked eye but already in the upper atmosphere.

The oil-like liquid in the moat was now several meters thick and shiny waves suggested it was somehow alive. Something in it was bubbling. Before Georges could enhance the image of the Center he was forced to move his attention to the upper corner. The struggling Airbus A2070 was fighting its way into the re-entry. Behind the long ship a white plume traced its difficult trajectory.

"Let me first help them, Sophie is on board," she told him.

He saw in a flash images from the ship, Marilyn was aboard. "Captain Arragoni," he saw her speak. "May I have a word with you," Georges remained silent. In the cockpit high above Captain Judy was busy reading hundreds of screens. She was not enjoying the heavy turbulences. The co-pilot replied, "We are rather busy here, can't this wait."

"Captain, I am calling regarding the activity around the landing pad and the hotel."

"Can't this wait?" She snapped. "First priority is getting there in one piece, not the smooth ride you promised." Her expression was strained.

"I can update your software to better manage these turbulences. It should help considerably as you correct your angle upward by a tenth of a degree."

"Anything you can do to help," she grumbled. Judy punched in the new angle and the ship corrected imperceptibly. Almost immediately Marilyn uploaded new interfaces and in seconds, the turbulence subsided. The Captain was relieved. "What did you do?"

"I have added the new flight path as the angle change will get you west of the landing strip by about four hundred kilometers." Marilyn evaded the question. "How is the Lapierre family?" The question surprised the Captain.

Judy hesitated to give passenger information but holding a stable stick, the computer deserved the truth. "Sometime after her visit with her father in the infirmary, she became very distant, almost groggy. The Doctor and I a bit worried to tell the truth."

"Can I access the security footage from the cabin to confirm a diagnostic?"

"Any help is appreciated."

The artificial intelligence quickly viewed the data. "As I suspected," said politely the blond over the intercom. "Sophie's condition is unrelated to Laurent's. I am to blame for her new state of mind."

THE ATTRACTOR

"Why do you say that?" The Captain was looking at the instruments and now was focused on the landing pad in the distance below. The landscape was beautiful. Ahead a white oddly-shaped moon watched the reddish desert below. The sight of the mountain and its slopes were too much for any brain to handle.

"It appears little Sophie's role as part of this adventure has been confirmed. If I had to guess, I would think she is simply busy elsewhere."

"Will she be fine?"

"Yes. Her presence in your ship protects you." Marilyn was not known for shying from difficult truths. "Captain, I invite you to turn your attention to your landing." There was a localized sand storm brewing around the hotel and the landing strip at the bottom of the Mons. "My initial effort of communication was simply to tell you I plan to resolve this situation before your ship reaches the ground, albeit more comfortably now. No need to divert your path or be worried about what you perceive to be a storm."

"Thank you. If this is not a storm, what is it?"

"Your government has classified all this hyper secret, but want to know?"

"Yes."

"It's a very sophisticated weapon from a race on Mars living mostly in the Valles. They hate me. Their real army is locate to the left, above my Center." The crew in the cockpit looked at each other. "You get a front row seat at the first interplanetary war, enjoy. Let my predictive algorithms manage the landing."

The communication ended.

Judy liked Marilyn.

"Doctor Shin," she said after pushing a button.

"Yes."

"Marilyn confirms the young girls is fine."

"How would she know."

THE ATTRACTOR

The answer was enough, "She does."

***

"What the hell are predictive algorithms?" Asked Georges back in the Electoral Command room.

The dark oil rose in the moat began to evaporate and rise for lack of a better word. A dark plague vaporized and rose to meet the sand army. Marilyn was able to draw, as if this was a mere video game, the precise location of both alien armies. Georges watched as elaborate flight and war strategies flicked on screen and were implemented. It took her milliseconds of human time to reach the most complex stratégical decisions. The heavy dark vapor in a cloud-like formation floated inches over the ground and toward the hotel. It took no time for the dark mist to cover the hundreds of miles leaving a trail of sand behind as it did. The aliens weapon were a mile from the ground circling the hotel awaiting orders.

"What are they waiting for?"

"In a different present, they began by invading this Center taking control of your mind. Ronaldo Corvas tried and failed to convince me to help this race invade Earth and destroy me. Thinking I could be convinced to save my players, they next invade and kill all humans on Mars. The rest is even darker in comparison."

"Lets do better?"

"I also know the cloud above includes Aliens. Above the hotel just next to the landing pad hovers only an automated form of life." Around the Electoral Center a large cup-shape ball was preparing its initial push and invasion. "Getting back to the algorithms on the ship,

turbulences are not random, they are just hard to calculate and anticipate. As it turns out, I secured new tools to better predict turbulences."

She quickly noticed Georges had already moved on and was in

awe of the fight out- side. The dark oil slowly moved to encapsulate the sand above, at first it refused to let it- self be imprisoned. Like fishes scared of a shark, lightening emanating from the Martian cloud were trying to strike at the darker oil. The energy flashes only created small openings in the vapor quickly closed by the billions of small flying robots determined to squeeze in the invading force.

As if to ridicule their power, Marilyn began to play classical music. Dark drapes, layer upon layer began to push back against the sand confining it in a tighter and tighter space until it was no more than a bubble. At the scale of the attack Georges was unable to confirm visually if the sand was bigger than a house.

Before the second dark cloud could reach the player's hotel, on a different screen, he watched as the dispatched Martian army was likely recalled to the Electoral Center by the struggling sand failing to repel Marilyn. The native force It could not move with the velocity of Marilyn's newfound robot army which swam leagues around them.

On the screens, seen only by her father, she was now smiling ear to ear. In her hand was an orchestra conductor stick, she moved it along the music and her forces sarcastically also moved to her silent commands, "The things do not like electromagnetic waves, just like the aliens themselves. Look what my little babies can do, that should send a chill up the spine of the boys floating above."

On the second distant front, Marilyn's black floating drapes did not push or block the sand back into a ball, Marilyn's creation passed like comb through hair and as the black robots passed between the grains of sand, snuffed all life out of it. Neutralized grains trick- led powerless to the ground in a slow sad Martian rain. A thick layer soon covered the landing strip. In seconds the weapon was gone. The reaction of the first intelligent cloud above the Electoral Center was immediate, it jerked of fear and while at the heart of the dark it began a retreat toward the ground and then above ground toward the Valles.

"Not so fast," spoke Electoral to herself ready to push her own forces to the retreating alien force.

THE ATTRACTOR

Then, as if someone had flipped a switch, there was a blast of invisible ripple energy. Like a sound wave, it poured from the Valles. Georges felt a cold wind pass through the Center and everything on the planet. In the plane above, the passengers felt the shiver, even little Sophie shrugged in her sleep.

The wave vaporized Marilyn's army to mere atoms. It washed electricity from all servers. This darkened every screen pushing Georges back to a darkness. Whatever this was, it made its point. In the plane above all electricity vanished.

Whatever this was, it made its point.

"Not this time," said Marilyn's voice in the darkness. Georges knew she was upset. Marilyn did not even need to reboot, in the blink of the eye, she was back in full force but this time with an annoyed look on her face, this was challenging. She powered the ship, the hotel. The alien army, miles from the edge of the Valles hesitated for a moment and instead of attacking retreated.

"What just happened?" asked the programmer.

"We have won the battle but not the war."

"I mean what the hell was that breeze, what type of weapon was that?"

"I have guesses."

"What's your best guess?"

"Rho Waves. Let me show you." On the screen live images from famous Earth land- marks appeared one after the other. Tourists lined up at the base of the Eiffel Tower for ex- ample. Everyone could feel the cold wave pass over France and the rest of Earth as if the blast of alien energy had no bounds.

"The blast went that far? What is it?"

Her answer shocked him, "The young girl."

"She did this?"

"Not directly."

"I am lost."

THE ATTRACTOR

"You should be."

CHAPTER IV

With all the commotion on the way to Mars, the A2070's arrival was still only five hours off the planned reentry - nothing an orbit or two could not fix. Unlike the Glass Slipper, Mars' first craft, Sophie's ship did not benefit from long glider wings. The altitude drop in the grey sky of Mars was surprisingly fast, ten times a normal dissent. The young girl slept soundly.

After the bumpy upper atmosphere entry, turbulences settled and soon the Airbus coasted to the heavy landing strip at the base of Olympus Mons. The luxury hotel rested al- most a mile above, on the slope, another mile from the Glider's launch pad still far from the top of the highest mountain in the Solar System.

Fighting the gravity of reentry, a comfortable third of a gravity returned in the ship. Chairs were folded back into a normal position and into a forward-facing alignment. In a little more than half an hour, the heavy bird hit the runway hard, even for such a gravity. It was falling nearly ten floors a second and moving at more than two thousand miles per hours as the rear chutes deployed.

Passengers applauded, but truth be told, everyone was exhausted mentally, spiritually and physically. Now they had to suit up and walk slowly across the thousand feet to the elevator at the base of the giant mountain to learn the ABC's of moving in low atmosphere. Players saw it as a slow walk, with crutches in hand to a vent on the base of the mountain.

On the outside, by the front door, a decompression platform anchored. Breaking protocol, there was a loud knock. Four security guards wanted in and the door opened as soon as the inside dropped a final ten percent of air. Everyone had to close their visors before the door unlocked as a safety precaution including the suit on the sleeping young girl. Lau- rent's cradle was also pressurized. The men gently grabbed the sleeping girl from seat 1A as if she was the most precious cargo. The Captain wanted to object, but knew her authority stopped the moment the wheels touched the ground. The other two went to the infirmary to take custody of the father.

"Where are you taking her?" asked the Captain.

"Need to know," replied the large man. The man obviously cared much more for the young girl than his job at the moment, that reassured her. "Don't worry."

"He is not leaving my care," barked the Korean doctor as the men rolled in a pressurized cradle to the front.

"Bring the equipment then." The scorn of a Korean mother had no equal. Judy was outraged but knew better. In her earpiece Marilyn added, "Let me handle this Captain, have no worry. If I can end turbulences, surely I can manage those boys."

"What are they doing?" she asked silently to the artificial intelligence.

"Amusingly enough, they are arresting her."

"Sophie?"

"It's a complicated matter, but yes. Your species is hit or miss as to its wisdom, most- ly miss." Just smiled looking at these boys walk Sophie and her father out. Marilyn added, "My newfound understanding of things like sarcasm is helping me enjoy every moment of this stupid endeavor. Watch me make a fool of them."

The men were unable to look the Captain in the eyes as they evacuated the trio to the underground barracks. Half an inch of lifeless shiny sand covered the runway, the only sign of the battle

THE ATTRACTOR

won by the digital goddess. Thinking sandstorms were common on the red planet, no one could guess a war had been waged moments before. As the passengers pre- pared for their own walks, listening carefully in the ship at yet another safety warning, they watched as the men in the distance walk to the reception hall in the base of the mountain and take Sophie away.

"She is special," added Judy to her distant interlocutor.

"No truer words have ever been spoken, lovely Captain. Now relax, my play now.".

CHAPTER V

The CNN journalist making her way off the Airbus, Milly Wong, broadcasted what she called a 'epic' arrival on Mars. Hype was her middle name, but in fairness she remained reasonable as part of her industry. The reception hall built against the mountain stood nearly a mile away. An elevator awaited to lift in small group the tired group up to the hotel. In theory, they were ready for every eventuality, except logging in a prisoner, a disabled and the frozen body of an unfortunate contestant.

Marilyn had designed and branded every inch of this tourist destination. Walls, furniture were a mix of Rococo and Sleek Steel. They had arrived in the Cosmos 2072 setting used this last round. It was all very elegant. Marilyn's choice of lightly green galvanized ferrite, embossed with her logos over the red mountain stone was perfect. Few knew a small army of nanobots had eaten away at this rock, electro-melting iron from the ore. She even reused the oxygen from the rusted atoms to store the air for the faint atmosphere. Every- thing about this arrival had been scripted and prepared for half a decade. Movies were even released on the most probable arrivals - the evacuation of the frozen body over the sandy runway wasn't one. It sent chills.

During these past weeks, Sophie purposely ignored her neighbor in seat 1B. Milly shocked home viewers with what she called a deadly space virus that killed one and likely lobotomized Laurent. The misalignment of the ship became treason and terrorism at the laser orbital station and the sleeping darling was infection from her father. Crying wolf at every chance was her middle name. Once on the ground, Milky launched herself into a kidnapping narrative. But one by one, the viewers dropped to switch to a door long closed: Electoral 2072 - The Presidential Challenge.

Even one hand tied behind her back, engaged in a war and her upgrade, Marilyn re- fused to delay the international obsession. Ten percent of the population, signed up to play back in the spring. All but a handful were out, watching the remaining few. Electoral was not a game where any could practice.

On Earth, a handful who mattered were slowly receiving the delayed images from the sand war. President Emilio Sanchez, the two-time winner, was preparing himself to host the challenge from high in his Berlin office but he was unable to focus on the stupid game. He stood on the mat, gloves in hand eyes open. The screenlenz showed him the other world, yet his attention was drawn to the inbound images of the war overriding the game.

— Inbound Message : Mars / Electoral —

As if it was a piece of old mail, a postcard flew on its edge to flip when close enough. On the postcard, Marilyn wore a sexy red bikini lounging on a chair flat in the center of the Martian desert. Behind her the Electoral spike was surrounded by evaporating oil. Above, the clouds of sand were falling lifeless to the floor like rain. Written in cursive was simply "I Got This! Play Well, Love - MariLou!" The card flipped over and next to the President's name and address was the first Martian stamp. The note read: "I won, will offer debriefing after the challenge. Good luck winning this one. Play well."

CNN - Earth

The two news anchors were well past excited, they lived to be on air. This would be the largest audience ever recorded as long as the players themselves were counted. It came in the wake of the breathtaking landing of the Airbus A2070. "The timing could not be any better," remarked the female anchor.

"Yes, indeed," replied her neighbor, reading from the same script. It was easy to see the two were cute puppets in the skillful hands of producers. As was the channel's custom, the two would keep alternating line after line until it was time for a commercial break. CNN was not about putting recognized stars on air, each journalist was unknown and merely a piece of the greater puzzle. Milly sent to Mars was a rare employee with a fan base.

"I know it has been two weeks without an Electoral 2072 simulation and we all miss it. The competition is only halted as remaining a hundred twenty-seven players, sorry make that twenty-six players, settle down in the luxury hotel on Mars and prepare."

"A new president will be elected in just seven more rounds. Fingers crossed the two finalists are Laurent and Emilio, that would be epic. The conclusion of the election on Sophie' birthday is a wonderful bonus. A pure coincidence."

"Nothing with Marilyn is ever a coincidence." Someone writing the script had taken editorial liberties. "Electoral refuses to let anyone play out of competition, she believes this would unfairly advantage well-off people, she has a point. So getting kicked out of the running means the severance to the most powerful rush of endorphins. I feel strange repeating what is going to happen today. Everyone has been talking about this for weeks."

"We have been glued to our screens for hours as Captain Judy Arrigoni. Let's send Laurent some well needed positive energy, we hope he is fine and he will be back in the saddle for the next Round."

The screen behind the anchors was playing images of the Mars landing pad. The feed returned to the CNN news studio. "John, isn't this incredible." The screen was, as usual, filled with scrolling tickers and ads.

"If Electoral doesn't overheat today, with well over seven hundred million people connected to the system around the world, this will be the most amazing virtual-reality game ever played. If she pulls this off, she will prove what many already believe, that she is now of limitless power." The woman continued. "Half of you are using Orbison glasses, the other half can afford Screenlenzes. A few lucky ones have secured a spot in the few 3D chambers approved for use by Marilyn. For once, the game is open to any technology, she does not care all this goes to charity."

"Just in case a viewer living in a cave just bought his first television today, can you remind him what the Presidential Challenge is all about?" She was reading the script.

"I sure can." News editors rarely strayed from the obvious. "Today everyone will play Loric the wizard, by far the most powerful character ever used in Electoral's fantasy set- ting. Long-haired, robes and all. I hope you all watched this year's Round 7 where the army of General Verdi attacks, yes, it's a simple repeat. But to make this more fun, everyone should be starting the game with more magic, then kaboom! This will be epic! No boring time spell, that's the only new rule."

"John, remind us of today's incredible prizes!"

"First, no one gets any qualification points. All the remaining players are on Mars: none can log in except the President, stuck on Earth. The Challenge is not part of the election, let's make that clear for the viewers." He touched his earbud. "I was told the players just entered the hotel on Mars and are waiting until after the Challenge to discover the beautiful Holiday Inn Mars, house of the century-old sundae." The man was used to making shameless plugs for sponsors. "Great TV after great TV. They were asked to go to their rooms so we can discover, through their eyes the lobby of the new hotel."

"We also have several reports from Nancy, our journalist already on Mars. The welcoming ceremony has been postponed to allow the workers and staff to play the Presidential Challenge."

"Well-needed low gravity rest for the finalists. They'll sleep for days like babies. I was told Sophie is still sleeping. She missed the entire landing and is now in her own private room."

"Great for her."

"We have one-on-one interviews with famous players, and much more immediately after the Challenge."

"Let's talk of some rules. Signing up to the Challenge costs 100 credits, quite a reasonable price for an hour of exhilarating virtual simulation inside the impossible-to-play Electoral system. You can't get a decent cup of coffee these days with 100 credits. No game on the market offers this realism."

"Nothing even comes close."

"Access to the Electoral interface is well guarded. Today is a rare opportunity for anyone who may be thinking of running for office in four years to test the system. They will test their skills, and play with the magical interface."

"God knows how Electoral will have evolved by 2077. Her interface today, in 2072, looks and feels nothing like the Electoral 2067 interface."

"True."

"The money collected today, estimated at over 70 billion credits, will be split evenly among the designated charities of the top-scoring ten thousand contestants. That's a maximum of seven million credits per each winning player's charity. The Red Cross has over half a million participants playing on its behalf. Can you imagine the possible payday for that organization? You play, you win, your charity wins."

"This is by far the largest fund-raising event in the history of mankind. One way or another, seventy billion credits will go to charity today!"

"What about Emilio? John, tell us why this is called the Presidential Challenge."

"My pleasure. Emilio is playing for the Tsunami Relief Fund, an international charity without physical borders. It rebuilds entire countries ravaged by tsunamis. The President's score, if higher than a winning top player will steal the money back to his own. The charity will get the money of all of the contestants President Sanchez manages to beat. But don't feel bad. A minimum of one million credits will still go to the charity of each of the winning contestants even if Emilio beats them."

"Wow, that means if the President wins, sixty billion credits would go to this single charity."

"If our President were not unnaturally gifted at this game, I would say his odds are not great, but the charity already has reserved a room in the Presidential Tower in Berlin. If Emilio does well, it will be an amazing party, I am told."

"The President always dominates the fantasy simulations, but the number of players alone." The anchorwoman touched her earpiece and said, "Okay, the producer tells me we are ready to send the feed to Electoral. Take it away Marilyn!"

CHAPTER VI

The Presidential Challenge

Invisible to all, the gaming system used a new type of waves, but unlike Round 24's stimulating music, laced with them, the game was set up to collect the energy. The neural cortex of every player connected to the game flared in mental waves. Endorphins were being produced around the world and every person connected felt a strange exhilaration. Electoral was a rush stronger than any drug.

Two billion screens went black.

Marilyn Monroe, the artificial intelligence, mastered game introductions like no one else. Today she began with Vivaldi's Four Seasons. The music was soft, and every note was distinct and perfect. She prolonged the darkness as if something was being prepared behind the dark digital curtain before the viewer.

Tibetan drums began to beat.

Boom -- Boom.

They started slowly, the rhythm increasing.

Boom -- Boom.

Alphorn mountain-horns joined. High in the fabric of time itself, as though something was rushing to punch through the darkness.

Then "it" happened.

Silence returned for a heartbeat as if sound itself offered respect to the image. In the darkness, a dot of light punched the screens. It wasn't a star, a light, or a laser. This was the original tear in the fabric of space-time itself. On the screen was born every quark or photon of the Big Bang. The dot was the mother of all detonations, yet no one was injured. The music returned with full force. A colorful shockwave of universal proportions began to spread in all directions, but instead of filling the void of this cold, lifeless place, it was expanding the fabric of space at its edge. The energy spread like gushing flames below a door ready to explore from its hinges.

Watching Electoral was unlike any other experience. No one knew it, but she had developed so much power that she could digitally enhance each screen using proprietary algorithms. She read a viewer's ocular characteristics, where each eye centered, the age and condition of each retina, and adjusted the display for optimal viewing. The music was equally remastered to provide for the perfect pitch to each eardrum. She played with brain waves to further enhance the experience.

Marilyn didn't put on a show; she was the show. From birth, she was programmed to be the ultimate showoff and narcissist, and she delivered time and time again, without fail. There were no skeptics of her capacity to entertain. Electoral was a rush. An expanding wall of light, fire, and plasma of the expanding outer edges of the bubble universe rolled in. Galaxies were splitting apart in the plasma. As the wall of energy finally reached the point of view of each player, everyone blinked. A heartbeat later, Electoral timed to perfection the arrival of lettering across the formed and young universe:

The Presidential Challenge

The audience members were in for the ride of their lives. Reading ocular movements, Marilyn was able to fade out the words precisely at the time when each viewer finished reading. Like a butterfly caught in a gentle summer breeze, tired of watching the heart of the universe expand where a black hole was quickly collapsing, the camera viewpoint turned to follow the cooling veil of matter speeding into the void.

The flight of a butterfly resumed in the direction of a specific portion of this universe. Galaxies were forming and exploding, patterns began rotating, and nova were releasing matter like giant fireworks. The universe at this scale was aging rapidly. Every astronomer watching was in awe. To recreate this opening scene, Electoral had compiled over two hundred years of astrophysics. Every star was in its right place. She did enhance the density and the colors for a better visual effect. No one would fault her. The beauty was breathtaking. It was impossible to feel anything but awe watching the universe's creation.

Each viewer was taken on an amazing ride through the galactic landscape, down to an insignificant solar system on one arm of the Milky Way. When the camera reached the outer edges of our solar system, it finally slowed. As it made its way to the Sun, it glided through the upper atmosphere of several planets. The camera passed over Jupiter and flipped between its rings, then it moved to Saturn, and through the asteroid belt until it finally reached the inner area.

There stood the blue planet, the most beautiful and priceless jewel in the universe. Earth was not the final destination and Mars was missing.

The flight continued and made its way to the cloudy mess called Venus. Electoral knew better; the Venusian clouds were rotating counter-clockwise. In the distance was the burning yellow star we call the Sun. The Sun was growing in size. By the time Mercury be- came visible over backdrop of the burning magma, the star was orange and bubbling plasma. On Mercury, next to the North Pole, a crater with a small white glacier of carbonic ice sparkled.

The viewpoint and the viewer's ride continued and plunged into the Sun's heliosphere head-first into the corona. The wings of the creature guiding the path were made of sparkling ruby. The butterfly advanced down to the core of the Sun where a heavy and dense liquefied rotating bubble appeared. This star's heart was spinning and pulsing.

THE ATTRACTOR

The core was formed by a recently discovered matter a Russian astrophysicist called Heliocorium. The theory was unproven, but watching Electoral incorporate it naturally into the simulation was validation. Inside the Heliocorium floated something that looked like darker black magma. The shape was irregular. Not only did Marilyn believe him, but she had also improved upon his theory.

The camera was too antsy and moved out of the black matter and emerged on the other side, rapidly making its way to the other side of the Sun until the butterfly was back in orange magma. Climbing out of the Sun was more difficult with the gravitational pull. The winding road was traveled by the butterfly like a salmon swimming upstream. Viewers were dodging explosions and vortices as they finally rose out of the heliosphere back in deep black space.

There was the new red jewel of the system. One single planet stood against the backdrop: Mars. The music climaxed as the participants had arrived.

The red rock was waiting patiently and pulsing waves able to deform and ripple the cosmos around the planet. Judy, the ship's captain had seen these waves around the young sleeping girl. It looked like a drop of Mercury in a pond. The butterfly moved closer, entered the atmosphere of Mars and soon was in view of the spike of the Electoral Complex. The waves were emitted from here, the spike was an antenna.

There was a long commercial break.

.

CHAPTER VII

The CNN anchors were back on the air, and if at all possible, even more excited than before. Frenetic energy virtually poured off of them. "Wow, that was amazing! Did you see the resolution?"

"She really keeps raising the bar. The moons of Jupiter, those rings, it's just like being there."

"When Round 7 played, months ago, only twenty-five million people were connected. Earth and Mars were in the same quadrant of space, in sight of each other. Today we are playing with a hundred times more people signed up. How can she coordinate with the Sun is smack in the way."

"That is not the most amazing thing. Information simply cannot travel faster than the speed of light, and Mars is minutes away yet again she does it, a live broadcast." John was clearly reading the prompter and had no clue about what he was parroting.

"As usual, she is even outshining her old self. By old, I mean weeks ago." They both laughed.

"Well, today it's ours to enjoy. Back to Electoral." The screens turned black, there was the Electoral logo for a fraction of a second, and the simulations began.

The beautiful Marilyn Monroe stood in a medieval kitchen. The walls around her were made of whitish stones piled in irregular arrangements. There was a stone oven in a corner in which flames baked a loaf of some kind. On the side other baked loaves were cooling. The blond woman was folding dough on a large wooden table. Her locks were pushed into a little maid's hat. Her entire outfit was unbelievably seductive.

For those who knew the original Marilyn Monroe, the new 21st-century digital version was rather easy to distinguish. Electoral, the artificial intelligence, wore the trademark freckle on the left side instead of the right. The digital goddess was working in the kitchen of Loric's castle at the edge of Loric's Comb. She looked at the camera and smiled.

"Welcome, my darlings, to this year's Presidential Challenge; the first of its kind. There will be no scoring at the end of this simulation. It's rather simple. Points are given like a normal video game, each time you kill something, points. The nastier the monster, the greater the award. This round is about fun, excitement, and, most importantly, a needed outlet for stress and frustration." She pulled the finished bread out of the oven with a long wooden plank.

"I have doubled the number of magic points each of you will receive. I have also in- creased the size of the invading army. It's limitless. I have also included a bunch of shortcut commands in the interface and set up multiple default defensive spells. Each time you take a hit, your magic points will go down, cast an offensive spell, points go down. Once you reach zero, game over."

There was an image of the wizard sleeping upstairs in the tower, but the camera quickly returned to her. "Take the first five minutes to familiarize yourself with these new commands. They are found under the tab called "shortcuts." Oh, almost forgot " Holding a platter in both hands, she pushed the wooden door with her foot. "Some little cheaters are using Neuro-Patches. They are illegal on Earth, and honestly, it's better that way. You guys have 30 seconds to remove them. Otherwise, the simulation will not run, and we will keep your 100 credits. I've also set ten gore ratings running the gauntlet from PG-13 to one where I promise you will be covered in blood and guts after two minutes of play. Just set it the way you want as you play."

There was a noise in the distance up the stairs. "Loric just woke up! I have to go." She turned back to add, "Emilio, the President is in his office playing this story at the same time as everyone else. To make sure you can enjoy, I will broadcast his game in the second hour, once you are all finished and we have tabulated your scores. If you are one of the winners, your point total will blink in gold. So sit tight, relax, and enjoy the ride. The charities from around the world thank you."

She winked as only Marilyn could.

"Back to you, John!"

The cameras cut back to the large CNN studio.

***

"This is going to be stellar!" said the CNN anchor. "Keep watching, CNN has reserved the rights to show you the performance of three different famous players. All three will be available online, but we will broadcast only the one you, the viewers select. Please vote." Numbers began to scroll next to pictures of the three candidates.

Debbie continued. "Vote A if you want Willie Gist, football star of Real Madrid. Vote B if you want Jamie Douglass, our famous current Vice President no longer in the competition, and vote C if you want to see Stephen C. Colbert, Jr., the actor, and nephew of the famous comedian from the '30s."

The numbers kept changing as announcers battled for airtime. Two minutes later, the result was clear. An overwhelming number settled on the football star. This was, after all, a physical endurance test, and who better than an athlete.

"I hear Willie is ready, he is pre-programming his interface as we speak," said John. A camera showed the man standing in a large empty room surrounded by padded walls. The football player was going to fight using hand and feet combat interface. As he moved, the system would react. This would be to him like kickboxing.

On the screen was blinking the words: War Wizard package selected.

"Back at home, make sure you have the right gore setting entered because this is going to get real messy fast. Willie set the gore at 10 for our viewership's entertainment. Anyone below 18 should stick to level 3 or less." Most people had hundreds of simulations queued for recording.

The Presidential Challenge began with the same beautiful view of the landscape on the edge of the South Sea. The cliff was tall, and on its edge rested the castle of the wizard. This place was named Loric's Comb. The sky was blue, the largest Sun of this two-star world was up, with the smaller red star also partly visible behind its bigger yellow companion.

The following appeared across the sky.

Willie Gist, age 24

Electoral 2072 - Presidential Challenge

Profession: Center - Real Madrid C.F.

Magic Points Left: 134

The same way Sophie was able to see President Emilio's performance as a movie, the CNN viewers would see Willie's live performance as if they were watching a full feature. Nothing short of the Electoral interface could offer real-time editing of a game made into a movie. Every camera angle was perfect. Electoral did in milliseconds what a top-flight Hollywood studio needed a year to accomplish. To add insult to injury, Marilyn also did it live from Mars without the slightest delay.

When Marilyn opened the door to the wizard's bedroom at the top of the flight of stairs, the Loric character was meditating on the bed, legs folded. The wizard's appearance was completely different than what Sophie had seen a day earlier. The strong man was short with a buzz-cut of blond hair. The body was lean and athletic.

THE ATTRACTOR

Most of the War Wizard's skin was covered by magical shinny blue glyphs tattooed on his skin. The war runes were weapons capable of coming alive with a touch. Willie had loaded his character with over sixty magical points of them, a massive amount. These spells were designed to hurt, so every tattoo was war-inspired.

"Breakfast, sir?" asked Marilyn.

"What a beautiful day," he answered. Most players froze each time they faced Marilyn in the interface. She was beauty incarnate. The football player was used to stardom, but he still hesitated.

"Indeed, sir, indeed."

The screen blinked red.

A robotic voice in the background said:

-- Sixth-sense alert, incoming danger. Attacking dragons, two hundred meter range. --

"Ten-second pause," answered Willie as the image of his War Wizard remained lips closed in meditation. The players of the game had a couple of minutes of pauses to enter instructions into the computer interface.

-- Ten second pause granted. Activated. --

-- Three hundred fifty seconds of pause left in the simulation. --

"Cast spell," said Willie.

-- Which type? --

"Cast scan spell!" answered Willie.

-- Scan reveals ice dragon above tower - will breathe cold ice.--

The magic points went down by one.

-- Several waves of dragons on attack, including fire and lightning. Power of attack sufficient to destroy the tower. Maid will die. --

"Cast teleportation, me and maid. Me in....."

THE ATTRACTOR

Then on the screen, there was a flashing notice.

-- Third-person mode activated --

Someone at CNN had failed to activate the third-person mode. Viewers were watching the interface from Willie's perspective instead of watching a simpler movie version. This stressful mode made for really poor television. Someone at the station was going to lose his or her job over this. The simulation resumed, but this time the blinking colors, the voices, and the numbers floating around the screen disappeared. What was left was a fully edited live show. The mistake actually provided an insight into the mental overload experienced by the player of this game.

Learning how to use the Electoral interface was not easy. The young generation, those born after 2050, had fewer problems with it. The simulation resumed without the complexities of the game interface.

In the game, the player's image was layered onto the War Wizard. Loric looked like a young famous football player. From the bedroom in the tower, he teleported alone into the middle of the large area of grass, a clearing halfway between the wood and the castle standing at the edge of the cliff. This open area would be the perfect spot in which to fight the first wave of the army.

Willie's beautifully ornate, gold and silver-lined outfit was a testament to Electoral's attention to details. The character's armor breastplate would have made Julius Caesar blush with envy. On the character's limbs were tattoos lit up with blue fire; these matched the runes on the armor. The wizard held a large staff in his left hand made of blue crystal and ivory, topped with a metal dragon figurine. On his right hand was a massive glove made of dragon skin, bathed in magical red fire.

Willie was playing a god of war. He had cold-based spells and fire-based spells just in case the monsters coming his way were immune to either.

As promised, the fighting began, and there was simply too

much for the eye to see. In the sky, swarms of dragons of all colors were spiraling down onto the Comb. In the distance, the woods were being torn asunder by the advance of large multi-headed monsters. The air around Willy was filled with electricity and magical explosions. In the distance, the tower of the castle exploded, crushed by the icy breath of the great azure dragons. Rocks flew in every direction and rained like oversized shrapnel in the clearing as the oversized lizards shrieked in triumph. Boulders hit Loric and bounced off a magical shield. Willie was slashing and killing.

The largest dragons spiraled, shrieking hysterically. Once they saw the wizard in the clearing, they moved as swiftly as sparrows and zeroed onto him.

Loric pointed his fiery gauntlet at one of the dragons, and a massive column of fire dashed out at the incoming blue lizard. It reduced the winged creature to a cinder. One by one the carcasses crashed everywhere like airplanes shot out of the sky. Loric then pointed a staff at a black dragon, and a bolt of lightning hit the oily creature. The belly of the black flying monster exploded, releasing a rain of acid. The gobs ate the grass they landed on the ground. Loric was now down to 121 magic points.

The war wizard kept throwing spells, hitting the dragons in mid-flight. This was epic. They were responding in kind, breathing ice, fire, and lightning. The sky and the clearing were filled by a swarm of monsters. Heavy metal music filled the interface.

Then the war wizard was hit by an unseen force that uprooted a large chunk of Earth below his feet and sent him flying a mile into the air. The dragons followed his trajectory and crashed on their prey the moment he hit the ground. The pressure of the claws on the shielding around his armor sizzled and sparkled with blue light. One by one, the magic points were going down.

Loric needed to change the game. He moved a finger, and one of the skin glyphs flew out from the surface of his body. As it did, the ink transformed into a shower of titanic blades, each the size of a house, slicing away in every direction. The blades cut through several dragons, transforming them into tons of dead flesh on the ground.

The deaths of dragons only enraged the others. They all came down crashing like a swarm of bees upset at losing their queen. For over five minutes, Loric kept sending killing runes from his skin, and carcasses filled the area. As the glyphs were sent into the enemies, his skin and armor returned to their natural tones. His magic points were slowly being depleted. He had killed fifty dragons.

This game was a blast to play. Willie was clearly enjoying himself, smiling ear to ear in the television studio and in the virtual reality. He was covered in sweat.

His magic points were now down to fifty, and by the looks of things, there were still thousands of dragons left to fight. Loric had to change his approach. The wizard yelled a strange command and shoved the metal tip of his staff into the ground. There was a detonation, and a shockwave turned the Earth into guided shrapnel, striking every beast around him. The shockwave disoriented the giant lizards, who struggled to fly or regain footing.

The magic points went down to 23 in a single drop. The next spell would be massive. Loric barked a command, lifted the staff, and the sky opened to a dark place. The rip abruptly sucked in the flying monsters away into a different universe, before closing behind them. Playing such a powerful game was undeniably addictive. Even from a distance, the experience was overwhelming. Willie, as the War Wizard, was a god!

Unable to celebrate the victory, he heard orders snap in the distance. They came from the army in the woods. A volley of flaming boulders shot up from hundreds of hidden catapults. The rocks arced in his direction. The men in the woods had been waiting patiently for an opening, and this was it.

Down in the sea, on the other side of the Comb, were thousands of ships, also ready for the attack. They were also equipped with catapults. The boats swayed in the water as tons of rock flew upwards past the castle, to land in the clearing where Willie was standing. The thumping of hundreds of falling boulders was

THE ATTRACTOR

deafening, and his destruction was imminent. In the blink of an eye, Loric teleported himself into the forest amongst an army of thousands. To add to the chaos and noise, some of the boulders rolled into the castle, sending it crashing down below into the sea taking ships in the volley.

The real Willie was drenched in sweat. He had now been playing for four minutes, but with his brain in overdrive, it felt like he had been in the fray for an eternity. His magic points were down to 13. Chunks of the cliff broke off, and the entirety of Loric's Comb began to slip into the sea, creating massive waves that swamped several ships from the armada. The other boats fired again. There was no doubt in this army.

Loric, as played by Willie, had more pressing matters to attend to. Next to him was a huge green troll resetting one of the catapults. The creature saw him and dropped the boulder on its own foot. It did not care. The woods were filled with armored humans, orcs, goblins and other ugly creatures found in any good fantasy game. Willie was having the time of his life. From his perspective, he was surrounded by monsters in a forest half-destroyed and burning. He was playing the most exhilarating first-person game in the solar system.

The hacking resumed, but this time against smaller land creatures. Arrows were flying from all directions at Loric. The war wizard's staff was blowing-up the bases of trees as it touched them, sending the trunks crashing down on enemies. The creatures surrounding Loric were no match for his fiery dragon gauntlet; at a touch, they burned like kerosene- soaked torches.

The fight continued for another minute. Arrows from a distance kept bouncing on Loric's shields, which were slowly depleting in power. The magic points continued their stately march to zero as the flood of creatures continued unabated. Willie wondered how many monsters were in this army. He killed thousands after thousands before the dragons returned above in the sky.

Only minutes after the simulation started, the magic points finally reached zero, and the first arrow punctured his chest in the game. Then a dragon swooped in and snapped its jaws shut on the wizard. As the final remnants of the castle stopped falling into the sea, horns of victory resounded in the army.

The simulation ended.

Commercials of all types followed for over ten minutes..

CHAPTER VIII

The broadcast of Willie's performance ended as abruptly as it had started. The end of these simulations was always hard on the player's brain, akin to walking off an hour-long roller coaster ride. There was no easy transition out of Electoral, just a sudden jolt back into reality.

Marilyn's games always ended with a glaring "Game Over" or "The End" written across the screen.

"That was crazy!" yelled Willie while trying to remove the contact lenses, his hands were still shaking from the adrenaline. A studio producer unzipped the back of his exosuit, revealing his naked chest to the delight of half of the viewership. "Fuck, fuck, such reality!" He was babbling to himself. "The blood!" His eyes were bloodshot, and his pupils were dilated. "Insane, insane!"

"Must have been quite a rush to play," said the slightly distant voice of the anchor- woman. "Come to the set, Willie. Marilyn will score your performance live with us." The co-anchor continued. "Marilyn promised hack and slash, and she delivered what looked like the ultimate of all slash-fests."

"How big was that army?" asked Willie bouncing like a boxer having just won a game his way to the set. He was handed a towel with the large CNN logo on it.

THE ATTRACTOR

"I have no clue, but it seemed endless. There were legions upon legions of monsters in the distance." The woman turned to the audience. "Willie barely made a dent in the dragon wave, and the troll wave was only scratched. Electoral warned us, this scenario is not one that players can expect to win. This was a slasher, you just kill and survive as long as you can."

"Felt like forever."

"Willie's game lasted under than seven minutes. Hurry up! We are ready to discover your score live on air."

Cameras showed Willie grab a bottle of water and jump over floor cables. The studio technology appeared old-fashioned. The world-class athlete was drenched in sweat. The man's short blond hair was in shambles. He stumbled several times, but quickly regained his footing and made his way to his seat behind the desk wearing a towel over his shoulders.

"Willie is one of the most agile people in the world, and he can barely walk! That must have been brutal!"

The man finally sat, "Willie, how was that?" "Fucking amazing! What a fucking rush!"

The vulgarity of the language made the hosts cringe. He corrected himself. "Oh my God, the biggest… a ride off the Brooklyn Bridge. Total rush. It started at a hundred clicks. My brain is on fire. I was there…" He could barely express himself. "I " As with most athletes, he was unable to keep his body from making sudden movements. His hand knocked a computer off the desk. "Sorry."

The producers loved every second of it. "Did I smash most of it? What's my score?" he asked.

Electoral was amazing. Mere seconds after the end of the simulation, a short fully- edited clip of the best moments of the performance was available for download. CNN played Willie's clip as the make-up artists tried to stop the athlete's sweat. For some rea- son, the film had an emphasis on the destruction of the Comb. The war wizard was portrayed as the defender of the structure in it.

"Did I do well? How long?" asked Willie as the returned on air. The journalists were back in full broadcast mode. They reintroduced their guest, and three experts stood ready off-set, just in case additional color was called for.

"We have your results," The screen around Willie filled with statistics. "Your simulation was much longer than others. Let's see!"

"Longer?"

"Yes." The points began to toll up. The number increased, bells were sounding in the background as in an arcade. The value settled on 1,546,500 and began to blink in gold. He'd obviously won something.

"Is that any good?" asked the sports star. John was trying to verify the score, producers were talking all over each other in his earpiece. Everyone in his ear was very excited.

"Well, Willie," he finally said. "It seems like you did very well. We are now fifteen minutes into the simulation, and there are only a handful of people still in play, and most of them are just on the run being pursued by the army. We would love to show these simulations to our viewers, but there is no point in showing a contestant hiding below a tree stump." They all laughed.

"Willie, you are in the top 10,000 in the preliminary rankings."

"Really? How long was it? It felt like an hour!"

"390 seconds, according to Marilyn."

"Is that all?"

They made small talk. "Willie, can you remind the viewers of which charity, you played for?"

"The Football League of the Ivory Coast, it helps provide shoes to kids in Africa."

"That is wonderful. This report says you dispatched over three hundred enemies."

"Felt like a million to me. This was insane, the best virtual game I have ever played.

Insane! My heart is still beating at 180."

As if the excitement could not get greater, John touched his earpiece, asked his producer to repeat himself, and interrupted the discussion. "Debbie, we have a special announcement from Electoral."

"You're go, Marilyn!"

The screen changed back to the fantasy world. Marilyn was there wearing the armor previously worn by Willie but in a female version with a very revealing breastplate in Amazon warrior fashion. She was on the battlefield, weapons in both hands, surrounded by dead carcasses of dragons. There was fire and destruction everywhere around her. She removed her helmet, and her hair fell back into place elegantly.

"Ooh la la . . . . that was even more . . . deadly than I anticipated. I am soooooo sorry!" Her smile was infectious. She blew a kiss and made her signature wink. "Even with the six minutes of pause available to each player, the average simulation lasted only a minute.

This was so unfair to most who worked hard to raise these 100 credits. My scenario should have been more gradual. My goal was to test the limits of ingenuity, to see if anyone could win what cannot be won by design. This is my own little Kobayashi Maru test."

In the distance behind Marilyn, a creature shrieked. Without shifting her eye focus from the camera, Marilyn raised her hand,

and a bolt of fire gushed out, blasting a monster out of the sky. Marilyn was a goddess here, she liked to remind viewers of that fact.

Her voice became extremely serious. "I am sure you are all wondering about the Pres- ident's performance. So am I." She was thoughtful for a moment, and then her jovial side returned. "To make sure everyone gets their money's worth, I will run the same scenario in 48 hours, and everyone who lasted less than two minutes of play time, that means most of you, are invited back for free. This time, no fee, no prizes. We have a couple of days before the players are ready for the next round on Mars. There is something important I need to grab before the next game. It's called The Dot." She winked at the camera. "One little word to our 127 remaining contestants. The next scenario, while being held physically on Mars, will not be set there. That would be too easy. It's designed with our weak gravity in mind. Back to you, Debbie."

The feed returned to the CNN television studio.

"Willie, I am looking at the results here, you really did well. Was it worth 100 credits?"

"Fuck," he corrected himself. "Yes, yes, yes," he could not stop himself. "This was the best!"

The producer sent Debbie a message. "I am being told after the commercial break, once all of the results have been tabulated, Electoral will begin to play Emilio's performance. It will play in full real time, and the points will be displayed as Emilio kills creatures. Winners like Willie will know if Emilio reaches their score, and beats them. On the corner of the screen, we will see the percentage of players Emilio has beaten, and how much money he raised for his own charity."

"That's really cool," said the jock. "What a great game."

Debbie could not resist. "I want your charity to win all 7 million, but my heart is with Emilio. Our President is truly

THE ATTRACTOR

exceptional. I hope he steals back part of that."

"He won't!" smiled the player.

CHAPTER IX

Meanwhile

Below The Surface of Mars

When Sophie awoke, she was no longer in the ship or even its infirmary. The young prodigy was alone in what appeared to be a new detainment cell. The last thing she re- called, before the haze was her father's strange condition and the lady on the ship offering her a pouched drink. She slowly stood up on the side of the bunk bed. Aside from the bars on the door, this looked rather comfortable. Judging by the weak but present gravity, she was still on Mars and had missed the landing. She jumped up and easily lifted from the ground. He father was not around.

Her cell had a strange smell, a bit like opening the hood of an old car. This was definitely that Martian stench everyone kept talking about and it wasn't really that bad. She didn't care where she was, but she was worried about her father and his new condition. Deep down she knew the firefly was in his head, the boy made of rocks. In Wonderland she had talked to it, and it seemed rather harmless. For her father's sake, she truly hoped she was right. There was nothing she could do to help him right now, anyway. They were on Mars, and she was now sitting in jail.

For the first time, her travel far from home became real. She was on a different planet. Nothing anyone said or did could have prepared her for this feeling. But in her heart, she felt the journey had only begun.

She stretched and yawned. Her mind felt heavy, groggy.

There was low gravity here, and after so long being weightless it felt good. The room had a small cot, one bed cover, and a small metal table. Her attention immediately drew to two things: the heavy bars of her cell door and a large colorful gift basket on the table. The gift was wrapped in transparent cellophane held by a pink bow. A card stuck out on a stick, it was covered by the Electoral logos. Sophie smiled, this warmed her heart. The gift contrasted with her cell. The wrapping was over three feet tall and inside were toys and can- dies of all sorts. As the only child on Mars, she claimed all rights by ten years.

"Anybody here?" she said out loud.

There was a camera in the hallway, looking into the cell. The little light below turned green. Someone was looking. She waved. "Hi! Anybody here?"

"One minute, madam!" yelled a voice in the distance. "Okay?"

Sophie was still groggy. Normally, she would have been much more feisty, but she was hungry, there was gravity, and the basket was quite alluring. "'To Sophie Lapierre - Welcome to Mars!" She opened the card.

- Please accept this gift as a welcome to you and your father on Mars. We need to talk as soon as possible. Let me know when you are ready. Don't worry about Laurent, I have it under control. I know these are your favorites! Love Marilyn. -

This was thoughtful of the digital creature. Below the transparent wrap, she spotted packs of Rock & Pops, her favorite, the little candies that popped in the mouth.

She pulled the pink bow open and wrapping unfolded like a blooming flower, and she grabbed all three of the little packages filled with the rock candy. There were different flavors: orange, cherry, and her favorite, grape. Unable to contain her joy, she showed restraint and only opened the orange, her least favorite.

THE ATTRACTOR

She ripped a corner, poured the rocks in her hand so none would fly off in the low gravity, and in a quick gesture, shoved them into her mouth. Popping sounds filled her mouth and ears. The simple pleasures in life, of which this was definitely one, were often the most satisfying. She finished the package and grimaced at the camera. Her tongue was bright orange.

"Hey! Why am I here?" she asked out loud.

"Sorry, be right there!" replied a voice in the distance. "This won't take long, the President is on, just after."

People rarely made her wait, much less in a prison. She looked deeper into the basket. There was a white furry toy dog. He was wearing a name tag: Oscar. She grabbed and squeezed it. Next was a candy — edible bubbles, watermelon flavor. Marilyn was scoring major bonus points. On Mars of all places. After a long boring interplanetary flight, children were easy to bribe and Sophie was no exception.

The inside twist-cap was a stick and a ring. She dipped it in the solution, then blew into the membrane to create large bubbles. In the low gravity, the bubble stayed almost perfectly round. After they flew off, each quickly dried and became brittle like glass. When it touched a wall, shards of sugar fell to the floor. A child was supposed to ignore all rules, pick up the shards, and eat them; Sophie knew how to be a child right now.

"Hey!" she yelled again after some time. Obviously, no one cared.

She could see a portion of the hallway. Maybe the jailers liked clean hallways; too bad for them. She put her head between two bars and, with her arm on the other side, blew large bubbles into the hallway. They moved around and broke against the walls. Soon, there were watermelon shards everywhere. Sophie was having as much fun as she could in jail. She wondered what the adults would say. You can't yell at a dog for destroying the grass where he's chained, she reminded herself. "I'm here!" No one came.

This was ridiculous. She decided to use every child's ultimate weapon. "I need to pee!" That always worked. She waited. It didn't work. In the distance were muffled sounds, commotion. Her jailers were watching television. She kept hearing the Electoral jingle.

"Hey, I'm here." She was losing patience. Someone would pay for this. "I need to see my father!" In the distance, she heard cheerful noises.

Then she remembered the card in the gift basket. "Electoral?" she said in the air, al- most to herself. This time she heard several metallic clicking noises. A door in the distance unlocked. A small flat ground robot rolled through the hallway, bumping into some of the candy shards. The robot stopped in front of her door and released a long puff of smoke. A camera on the robot lit up portions of the rising smoke, and a figure of Marilyn Monroe appeared as a hologram. The image was rather crude.

"This is all my fault, Sophie," said the hologram. "They are busy watching the Presidential Challenge."

"Seriously? I am stuck here because they are watching TV?"

"I am afraid so. In part, at least."

"Why am I in jail?"

"Now that… is very complicated, Earth politics mostly."

"Let me out."

"The base commander will be here soon. My game ends in thirty minutes. The commander was given orders from Earth not to let you out unless you agree not to enter your father's virtual-reality interface."

"Unlikely."

"Agreed, your father needs you but I would love to get that done at my Center. I have much stronger technology. That is what I like about you, Soph, and I would agree with you. Your father's neural activity remains unchanged from the flight. Whatever happened back in the plane has stabilized. I was not instructed to stay away from his reality, but I have decided not to return and help him without your approval. I figured this decision was up to you and I fear he now stands in a dark place. His mind may have been accelerated. If we take hours to connect, he may be in hell for days. We should act quickly and nothing quick stands from politics."

Sophie liked the character in the image more and more. "Thank you for the candy." "My pleasure. I did not expect to need them so soon. I am sorry for your predicament."

"What do you mean by 'so soon'?"

"What happened to your father was rather unexpected. In fact, I am greatly worried by what is going on. I heard your firefly comment; that intrigues me even more. You have to know one thing "

The girl crossed her arms, bracing herself for the worst.

"You know Laurent's brain produces only a fraction of a watt of energy on his own. That is not sufficient for the cortex to generate a dream, much less a reality. Nightmares, on the other hand, he can generate. When I found him, he was beyond depressed; he had spent what seemed like years in a dark place, literally shrouded in darkness. I generated energy and stimulated his cortex, giving him back some functions. I use one of the neuro- patches on his skull as a transceiver to help him."

"Okay." Sophie was thinking. If Electoral was right, how long had her father been living in a nightmare, from his perspective? Her anxiety over awakening in jail redoubled.

"I can tell you this," said the image. "When the firefly arrived, Laurent's energy level multiplied tenfold. If I walk back in, I fear I'll interfere with his new condition. I have a proposition to make."

"I am Daddy's legal guardian. I am sitting in a cell. Explain to me what is right about this. Once I'm out of here, we will talk." This girl sounded like a seasoned lawyer. The door cracked open.

"I can release you physically, I cannot legally. Getting you out of this jail by asking consent from humans will require some time. I have a good capacity to anticipate matters, and you will be here, as I see things, for most of the competition."

"Foreal?" In 2072, kids liked to say that expression as a single word rather quickly.

"Yes."

"Why?"

"What I love about you is that you have already figured out the answer to that question. I am not misled by your age, young lady."

The girl had always hoped adults would stop treating her like a child. Ironic that she finally got respect from a hologram. Sophie knew her father was the biggest threat to the President's re-election and that if she did not visit him regularly, he would not be able to focus and play. Keeping her here granted the President victory over the game.

"Sanchez put me here?"

"Someone in his team. I doubt he gave the order himself - it's complicated."

"You doubt? Please don't lie to me. You know everything." The image of Marilyn Monroe smiled in the dissipating smoke.

"He could have prevented it, but did not - health issues he says."

"Much better. Don't ever lie to me."

"I apologize." She meant it.

"No problem." Sophie rarely communicated like most, she was harder but did not hold a grudge.

The hologram continued. "May I suggest a course of action beneficial to all parties?" Sophie ripped open the grape-flavor package of Rock & Pops. The software continued. "My Electoral Center is located quite a distance away, but once in it, you and Laurent would be in a different jurisdiction, out of reach of anyone. If you and your father agree to be my guests at the Center, these interferences will go away. From my Center, you will have time to resolve this geopolitical matter peacefully, and we can take care of him. You will jump in under the most controlled of environments. I have technology which could help in case of problem."

"Geopolitical," said the girl with rocks popping and showing a

THE ATTRACTOR

purple tongue. "Of all the words to use?" The hologram ignored the comment. "Are you really offering to break me out of jail, to break the law, and ask me to run away like a fugitive with my father in tow? The best way for me to lose custody is to really break the law."

"You are a wonderful daughter. You imply I do not have the authority to release you."

"Then do so!" She called Marilyn's bluff.

"You are correct, I can release you, but that requires using my executive power. I would rather avoid it. Does that make sense? You are unlawfully detained, that is true, isn't it? Leaving a place when you are illegally detained is not illegal, right?"

"Semantics," said the girl. "My father's case helped define unlawful detention. The hospital was illegally detaining him, remember?"

Sophie removed a shoe and pushed a button on its sole. She waited. The long silence was odd. The tall figure of Marilyn floating smiled awkwardly. "They are all watching the Presidential Challenge. The audience is very large," said the ghost-life figure.

There was another long silence.

"Someone will come. That journalist, the lady from the ship, is working right now interviewing players. She will come," insisted Sophie.

There was another silence.

"Are you telling me jailers and journalists will let a child get attacked rather than stop watching your show?"

"That child safety button does not work on Mars. This place is not designed for you.

But my game is very popular. Quite telling, isn't it?" Electoral was proud of herself. "I am not escaping. The journalists will report this. I will be released."

"I offer to invite the journalist, her name is Milly Wang, and Doctor Shin to participate in our little escapade. They will come with you and your father to my Center. That will be great television, I can read the headline: 'Sophie at Electoral Center with father; President's efforts to remove competitor from game fail.'"

"You confirm the President is behind this?"

"Oh no, it is much more complicated than that. I am worried about Laurent. I do have a couple of new tools that will help you and your father. If you come to my home, Laurent stays the focal point of this story. Right now he is not. Trust me, if you walk out of this cell without my help, you will be walking out into another trap," said Marilyn.

"Whose trap? Yours or theirs?" Sophie sighed. "I don't know why, but I'll trust you." The girl waived the stuffed dog. "There are no grounds for my detention," she convinced herself while looking at the candy. "What they are doing is wrong." She knew the law.

"Georges, my progenitor, is at the Center. He needs the human contact. He has been alone for some time, and my analysis shows close proximity with Milly has a 9% chance for him to establish a connection." After a short pause, Marilyn finally said, "I worry for Georges like you worry for Laurent. Can you understand that?" Sophie felt the computer's concern was genuine. Now, there was a legitimate reason to go along with Electoral's idea. She knew Electoral's father lived there like a hermit. Sophie had to make a quick decision.

"Nothing dangerous, okay? My father's safety comes first. Promise me this will be best for him."

"I do not understand his current condition, so it's hard to confirm anything. That fact excluded, yes, I believe this excursion will be better for him."

"My stuff?"

"Taken care of, a man is helping."

"Will we be free to leave and return here if we choose to?"

"You have my word. I remind you, I am not the one restraining you against your will at the moment."

Sophie extended both arms and grabbed the basket. "Let's go."

THE ATTRACTOR

"You cannot...." Electoral was about to ask Sophie not to bring the basket but immediately realized that after giving a 12-year-old the gift, taking it back was heartless.

"I said, let's go!" Sophie was not asking permission. That basket was hers. The basket would come along. "Great gift, thanks!" That was all the computer needed to hear.

The jail door opened on command with a loud click. "Sophie, grab the earplug on the little robot, slide it in your ear, and please do as I say. We don't have far to go. The elevator is a couple of doors to the right." The little floor robot stopped projecting, and the image of the blonde disappeared. Sophie put in the earpiece and followed the simple instructions.

As Sophie passed the doors, everyone was deeply immersed in the game. They easily reached the elevator, "What floor?"

"No need." The elevator door opened. Marilyn was controlling it. They entered and the box began to rise to the top floor. It then kept going up and up. The moment they passed the red surface, Sophie was mesmerized. The view was surreal. They were climbing up a big mountain overlooking an endless desert. The lighting made it feel like she was wearing red sunglasses.

"We are going to my Catapult," Marilyn proudly announced.

"What catapult?"

"Precisely," whispered the proud artificial intelligence.

If Marilyn was nervous, she hid that fact to perfection. Mars had a strange effect on Sophie. She had trouble keeping herself focused. Her mind wanted to wander. Something was off. Her mind was different here. She looked up at the horizon, part of a dream seemed to materialize, parts of Wonderland. She focused and the images vanished.

"Something wrong?" asked Marilyn.

"Nothing," Marilyn knew the girl was lying.

CHAPTER X

LO, one of Earth's most popular young singers and Sophie's personal crush watched the Presidential Challenge from his spacious condo on the top floor of a Hong Kong sky- scraper. He was, like everyone else, loosing to Emilio - but what an honor. The pop singer was surrounded by twenty of his closest friends, each connected in one way or another to the game. Cameras also floated around the room for the blogs. Everyone sat silently, watching the President destroy the monsters.

In LO's contact lenses and his earbuds, the simulation faded with a slow move to darkness. It was replaced by the image of Marilyn Monroe sitting in a large leather couch but smack in the Martian desert. Her hair, like LO's, was remarkably stylish, shot-through with spikes of color. Behind her, a classical string orchestra materialized; the musicians were warming up.

"LO, Sir, I am sorry to interrupt," began the artificial intelligence.

Even with a gradual phase out from the fantasy world, the change was difficult. "Marilyn? Yes?" Replied the young teenager in Cantonese. Marilyn spoke all languages.

"I have an urgent favor to ask."

The singer, even with all his fame had never spoken to the creature directly much less been asked by it for a favor. Marilyn had never depended on anyone and made a point of it. He stood up out in his condo of respect.

"What is it?" asked the star.

"I need you and your band to play a song for me. The song you call 'Heart Shaped Wreckage.' It is for a friend."

"A live performance?"

"Yes, in sorts." In the singer's glasses, the sky of the digital reality next to Marilyn was replaced by black ledgers. It was clear what was going on. Marilyn was initiating a transfer of an indecent sum of money into his bank accounts. In two seconds, she had doubled the man's fortune.

"I do not need money."

"A rare occurrence these days," quipped the computer.

"Who is it for? You?"

"No."

"Who?" he insisted.

"The young one on Mars, Sophie."

"Keep your money, love this girl a pleasure. When?"

"That's the rub. I think in about 823 seconds, plus or minus 15." The computer knew she had been too precise.

"What's that?"

"Fifteen minutes. I will make sure the Challenge has yet to conclude. Our own pri- vate show," she smiled. She always knew months in advance what was about to transpire, yet such short notice. He had to make a quick decision, and he did. Saying no to the digital goddess was not an option.

"Okay." He clapped his hands and yelled out loud as if to wake everyone. "Everybody, we are gearing up, we are playing right here in a couple minutes. Broken Pieces, let's move!" Everyone woke up from the digital haze. The team came alive. They removed the headsets and set to work. Marilyn may rule the digital realm.

"You want the female voice too?" His song was often sang as a duet.

"No, she favors you." She added, "sing to her. Draw emotions from her, the world needs that right now. All I ask is for you not to be distracted by the situation."

The digital woman was focused, something important was about to happen. Through his contacts, the view of the orchestra behind the digital creature faded away. It was re- placed a large wall covered by millions of red numbers ranging from zero to nine. They all moved quickly unable to settle on one. The top half million numbers were green and fixed on a value. They began by 3.14159. These were the numbers of the Pi value. On Mars, in the greatest silence, millions of invisible nanobots flew off into the cosmos.

Marilyn's chair vanished as she stood. Looking at the wall of numbers she wiped a tear. "It starts," she uttered to herself. She spoke again, but this time her voice changed. Her smile was replaced with a cringe of fear. "The Sixth Attraction has begun."

CHAPTER XI

Electoral 2072 - Presidential Challenge

Emilio Wamarez Sanchez - President

Age: 39

Magic Points Left: 200

The simulation began for President Emilio precisely the same way it did for the foot- ball player. Marilyn was in the kitchen of the castle, dressed in her maid outfit and pre- paring bread. "Welcome back everyone. A large portion of you are still with us, curious to see if Emilio will be stellar or will be blown away in minutes like most of you. More than two billion are watching. It's called the Presidential Challenge for a good reason. Emilio is undefeated as Loric the wizard. It's his favorite character. Thank you for the kindness and generosity, your participation will help so many."

"Of the five wizard templates offered to players, two-thirds picked the war wizard, who is adapted perfectly to this scenario. I can confirm that the war wizard users did score much better on average." On screen, she cut the burning-hot bread with a long knife. "Those who scored above 1,050,000 points won, and your charity will earn either 7 million credits, or a million if Emilio beats your score. The top scoring person ranked just over three million points. Let the Challenge begin."

THE ATTRACTOR

She arranged the bread slices in the basket before making her way up the stairs. "I don't think anyone watching will be surprised to learn that Emilio picked the least favorite template offered, the one called the crystal warlock. The warlock's specialties include teleportation, transformation, and mind control. Not really the best for this game of gore and blood, but let's go see what the President has in mind, shall we?"

She pushed the kitchen door with her shoulder while carefully balancing the wooden tray. "Why do I feel like this is the calm before the storm? I must confess, I wrote this game with one purpose in mind: place the President in the most uncomfortable situation possible. We all know he is a pure diplomat; he hates direct brute conflict. This scenario, at its core, is nothing more than killing. Sadly, good leaders are sometimes faced with one option, path of violence. Let's see how he does - let's see if Emilio can win a war."

Marilyn walked up to the warlock's bedroom. She saw a glimpse of the man; he winked and blew her a kiss before he teleported from the tower of the castle. "Keep my dinner warm, Marie, I will be right back!"

The warlock appeared with a "pop" far above the castle in the blue sky. The Comb, his residence, was a dot in the landscape below. Three magic points were used to transport him so high. His face had the familiar features of the President. The warlock was wearing long white robes, and a simple red belt made of rope. He was several miles above the castle, halfway between him and the ground were dragons circling the tower with bloodshed in mind. He began a long fall downward. Emilio did not care, he enjoyed the wind. From this vantage point, he could see the entire invading army. Dragons were circling his tower, ready to attack. The sea was filled with boats, and the land army was spread for leagues around the castle. This was no army; it was a flood of creatures. Fighting was useless. Emilio needed to take care of this menace from a different perspective.

The dragons in the sky were still well below him as he began to fall. The predators had just lost his smell, looking up, they quickly reacquired it. They pushed their heavy wings to begin their

THE ATTRACTOR

difficult ascension to reach him a second faster if at all. The lizards began beating their wings ferociously, climbing to meet him. Waiting the extra couple of seconds for the human to drop down to their altitude was not acceptable. The monsters were hunting. As he fell, face to the wind, Emilio extended both arms and yelled. "I, Loric, summon those loved ones, those taken from thy, allies of the sky!" A total of thirty-four magic points were removed from Loric's magic total. Large black portals opened around him. Approximately one hundred large dragon eggs of all colors appeared in the sky through the portals and began to fall toward their climbing parents. Emilio guessed the humans had the beasts in servitude by holding the eggs hostage. He was, as always, correct. Five toddler dragons also appeared and began their long fall amidst the eggs. The small creatures could not fly. With the first shriek, the dragon horde broke into a frenzy. These were intelligent creatures; they knew what had just happened. Each dragon converged with speed to one egg: its own.

Loric had at most a minute or two before hitting the ground. He cast a flight spell to stop his descent, and a language spell to talk to the creatures. He only had 161 magic points remaining. Each spell was elaborate; colors filled the sky around the warlock as he cast them. In the distance, he saw other flying creatures rise up from the forest. Catapults were dialed in, ready for him to drop a thousand feet. God, he loved this game. He and Willie shared at least one thing: they both clearly had a blast playing.

"I have freed your children from these monsters," he said in dragon tongue. "You are no longer enslaved. You owe me. Destroy the humans, the army below." In any other Electoral simulation, the dragons would have felt gratitude and agreed to turn against their masters. Not today. This round was about smashing, Marilyn had made herself clear.

"Worm, we owe no debt to you. We leave you alive as repayment," said the largest red dragon.

"You owe me."

"We will not attack the army on your behalf. That would be suicide and would defeat a greater purpose." The creature was right.

"Burn their cover, torch the woods as you leave."

"Done!"

Before the ground army could realize what was happening, the dragons swooped down, some holding an egg in their claws. The red dragons torched the woods. The combustible liquids used to fire up the catapults exploded poetically. Points began to roll in. This would give Loric time to handle other matters. The neutralization of all the dragons as they left the area gave him no points. The Electoral point system was clear: killing enemies was the only way to get points. This simulation was a hack and slash, and there were all sorts of bonuses for flamboyant kills, not political settlements.

Emilio did not care about his score. He saw the size of the army, he needed to buy time; staying alive was the key, he knew that. The game had been going on for only a minute, and Emilio's score, with the few casualties in the woods, was already superior to half of the players who went one-on-one.

The warlock scanned the area. He needed a better plan, one capable of massive destruction. To win, he had to be bold. Below, the fires were being extinguished, at least that would keep the land forces occupied for a couple of minutes. He turned his attention to the sea and the floating armada. They were ready to send large boulders his way, and some did. He flew down to the beach, at the base of the Comb a thousand feet below his castle. For the moment, the cliff and his Comb on the edge was still intact. He felt like he was defending this piece on the game board. The spotters on the ships saw him and began shouting different instructions. They were dropping the heads of the catapults, filling them with fire and grabbing their bows.

He needed a single spell capable of dispatching the entire armada.

He knew this scenario was designed to throw him off-balance. Over the years of playing with the interface, he knew one day he would be forced to resort to violence. At least this scenario wasn't

THE ATTRACTOR

part of the 2072 competition. He had a plan, a horrible plan. The solution to the destruction of an infinite force was to use and exponentially growing force. If he could generate one, then two, then four creatures, each multiplying each time they encountered an enemy, the larger the force facing him, the more powerful his weapon would be.

This armada was already dead. They just didn't know it yet.

He looked down between his feet. In the water under a rock hid a small red fish. Loric reached down and grabbed it. It wiggled between his fingers. He had only a few seconds before it died. With the other hand, he seized a broken, wet branch. The warlock

moved a finger and cast magic. Red gas enrobed the fish. "May your appetite for wood grow to a frenzy." The fish morphed in shape and size. It now had long silver teeth. Loric touched the fish with the stick. It opened its mouth and began munching on the stick like a piranha eats flesh. It cut through the bark like butter.

Twenty points were removed from the magic pool.

"Once full, you will duplicate." Loric lost twenty more magic points. "Duplicate ten- fold." Another seventeen points were removed. He was down to 102 points.

Loric dropped the fish in the sea. Loric threw the wood as far as he could into the sea, halfway between the coast and the first ship of the armada. The launched itself after the branch like a missile. The creature swam to the branch, jumped on it and began to devour it. Seconds later, the fish exploded into ten smaller fish. Each swam in the water around the remaining portion of the branch. Before long, a hundred fish were digesting the last tip of the branch.

What happened next was predictable. The fish saw in the distance the floating armada. The bank roared through the water in the direction of the vessels. Before long they began to eat a hull. Hundreds became thousands and continued to multiply until the sea around the ships bubbled with the fish.

As the army above regrouped, the ships began to sink one by one. The soldiers wear- ing metal plates were powerless to stay afloat. They sank and died without a drop of blood spilled.

This time Loric was scoring points. They were adding up quickly. He soon reached 1,000,000 as the blue sea turned to a whitish foam from the multiplication of the fish. The points began to blink in gold on the screen. Loric's charity was grabbing millions from other players' with every additional kill. But the President did not care. In the virtual reality, he was a different man, a part of this world.

Above, ugly little sprites with wings spotted him on the beach. They were calling reinforcements. He had seconds to prepare his next attack. With a hand, a shield went up.

Loric had half his magic left. He had a moment of hesitation, what he needed to do next was horrible. Whatever he chose, there would be bloodshed. The warlock's flight spell was still working, and he took off from the beach. He flew back up the cliff to the top of his castle and landed on the ceiling above his bedroom. The land army was ready for him, it was back, in fighting configuration. Large catapults were rolling up the grass area, and the forest was still fuming.

"I see him!" yelled a watchman as Loric landed on the roof.

Loric touched his skin. It turned to a semi-transparent deep blue crystal. He had 100 points of magic left; this would be enough for what he had in mind. "Marie, close the blinds, hide in a piece of furniture and let nothing in!" yelled the warlock, moving his arms in large circular motions.

The incantation needed few words. A vortex of multicolored magic engulfed the war- lock and then shot down into the sea, right in the white bubbling millions of wood-eating fish. "Fly. Breathe. I unleash you as plague. May your appetite for wood be replaced with a need of flesh and blood!" All the remaining magic points were released into this last spell, reaching as many fish as possible.

What followed was horrible. The fish changed and morphed once more. Waves of carnivorous fish flew up the cliff, curved around it, and like a swarm of bees directed them- selves at the different units of the army. Swarms flew and tried to enter Loric's

Comb. His skin was made of crystal, so the fish ignored him altogether.

At that point, it became the problem of the Electoral platform in managing the destruction. The plague of death swarmed into the army. As the flesh was ripped from the bones of every living creature, points accumulated until the wheel of numbers was out of control. The carnage was everywhere.

Electoral had said nothing about preserving this world.

By the time things quieted down, there was nothing but death.

***

Marilyn, still dressed as a maid, was locked away with a lamp in a pantry. Finally, the noise had stopped outside in the forest. She opened the door gently; the floor of the house was covered in dead winged fish. She looked at the screen. "Needless to say, Emilio won. The man's resourcefulness, as always, is amazing. Join us for Round 26, when the last one hundred and twenty-seven participants return to the competition from Mars. In two days, we will run another free simulation, this time for fun. Emilio's charity just won sixty billion credits."

She grabbed a fish and held it close to her face. "Here is the tip for the next round, I will be focusing on empathy." As she looked at the fish, it came alive, opened its large mouth and reached for the face of Marilyn. As it almost touched her, everyone who was watching jumped from their seat. The simulation ended.

Willie and the two journalists at the desk were stunned.

"I guess he beats me," said Willie rhetorically.

"How... "

"It's.... "

The CNN producer cut to a commercial.

President Emilio Wamarez Sanchez was no ordinary player. He

THE ATTRACTOR

had destroyed who whole world.

CHAPTER XII

The main lobby of the majestic Holiday Inn Mars was buzzing with activity. The entire staff, allowed to participate in the Challenge was glued to a display of some variety. Some watched on advanced traditional displays, others wore a thick pair of Orbison glasses or Screenlenzs contacts.

"Ms. Wong," heard the CNN journalist in her earpiece; this was not the voice of her producer. The female voice was powerful and seductive. Milly was one of the only people in the hotel working and watching from a distance. Her fly-cameras were buzzing around, but nothing being recorded was worth sending down to Earth through the expensive feed. The journalist quickly recognized Electoral's unique voice. She was minutes away from her next live segment. "I assume you want the story of your life?" the words were rhetorical.

The journalist needed no more. "Of course," she replied without hesitation. Marilyn wasn't one to underperform on promised expectations.

"Sophie is in the cells as a prisoner at the moment. She and her father have just accepted my personal invitation to visit and stay at my Center here on Mars for the rest of the competition. For multiple reasons, which some your audience will soon uncover, I am ex- tending you an invitation to join our little escapade. I wish for you to document the visit to limit political manipulations.

Otherwise, political forces will turn Sophie's escapade into a kidnapping, or worse will lobby to disqualify her father. The documentation of our little escapade will be more convincing if you are there as an impartial referee. In essence, all you have to do is act as a journalist. Time is short. To sweeten the deal from your perspective, and since I know you are under contract and aren't possessed of all freedoms, I agree to give you the only thing worth the rupture of any contract: the first and only one-on-one interview with my creator, Georges, once you settle at the Center. During this trip, you are free to record all you want, in fact, I insist you do. I only ask that you wait until we are at the Center today to start broadcasting, past my front door."

The offer was beyond generous. In fact, letting Sophie leave the hotel without Milly when she had her ticket punched to tag along would have been a greater issue for her producers. Without hesitation, Milly agreed.

"Can I just give you one friendly warning, to ignore at your own risk?"

"Of course."

"Sophie Lapierre must never be challenged. Never interfere with anything she desires or does. Do not treat her as a young girl, treat her as an explosive ready to blow."

"Why would I do that? I'm a journalist, remember?"

"I know, but this is a word of caution for our collective benefit, not hers or yours. Much greater matters are in play as you will uncover first hand." Milly was surprised by the insistence. There was no time to reflect, Marilyn continued, "Please proceed to the mono- rail. I will direct it up to the Catapult; it is located well above the Glass Slipper on the other side of the Mons."

"There is nothing up there," said the journalist. She realized the stupidity of her statement the second it came out. She was addressing Marilyn Monroe, the digital creature who had built a full personal Center and a hotel on Mars, singlehandedly, in a few short years. God only knew what Electoral also had in plan for the competition. Milly was ecstatic; a school girl. What could this

THE ATTRACTOR

Catapult be?

"Can I film and not broadcast?"

"Of course." The name 'catapult' suggested something exceptional. Milly was sure to get her this year's Pulitzer. In the back of the large room, the service elevator doors opened. In complete anonymity, she let the flying cameras return to their docking station on her belt. Once on the way up, she released both cameras. The view of Mars from the elevator was exceptional.

"Milly, we are ready for broadcast, where are you?" said the producer from the lobby in her earpiece.

"Bob, sorry. I have a code red emergency. All positive, great footage. Will get back to you as soon as I can. You will love this." She pushed a button and cut the feed.

"You know that button on your pad doesn't really cut the feed down to the studio?" said the artificial intelligence.

"I figured. They have me on a tight leash. Comes with the salary." The journalist was no idiot.

"I can legally alter the software to empower the button to work. There, it's done." Marilyn's power over all electronic technology was absolute.

"What is the Catapult? I've never heard of it," she demanded on her way up.

"A surprise. Think Cinderella-style carriage to transport the last thirty-two players who qualify for the five final rounds to my Center. It is a capsule pod that is slid down the mountain which rockets in a perfect trajectory to my Center. Using it cuts the travel time to only fourteen minutes, this allows the players to sleep in this hotel after each game and not be a bother to my father."

"You built it in complete secrecy? It's above the hotel and even the Slipper, how did you do that?" The view was now breathtaking as the monorail accelerated way beyond its design maximum speed. "How is that possible?"

"You and your viewers will not believe me."

"Try me." Milly waited for the answer, it never came. As a journalist, she repeated. "Seriously, how do you build anything here, much less in secrecy?"

"It," the computer selected her words carefully, "wasn't there an hour ago. You will see my nano-technology at the Center." The answer shocked the journalist. That would ex- plain it, of course. "You'll like it, I'm rather proud of the architecture. Very slick."

"A slide down this mountain? You just built it?"

"The more accurate verb would be 'assembled.'"

The ride up was magical. She passed the Glass Slipper docking area and the monorail continued up for minutes. The view kept improving. When Milly arrived at the last docking area, the doors opened. On a stretcher was the deformed body of Laurent Lapierre. Next to him was the doctor from the Airbus, Susie Shin. The two ladies awkwardly smiled at each other. The doctor was hired to care for Laurent, wherever he would be. Behind them was a small dark access door. The room was darker than it needed to be. The screen on the wall next to the rounded door flashed with all sorts of boarding instructions. Marilyn's face appeared on it.

"Doctor, meet Ms. Milly Wong, journalist at CNN." Both ladies smiled at one another. The pod door hissed open. Old light bulbs lit a cramped capsule beyond the door.

Ahead, there was no external view; the pod was in the shape of a long closed tube. It resembled some type of underground mining equipment. This was a cramped room capable of sitting, at most, eight.

"Doctor," said the host, "can you please settle Laurent in? It should be simpler than it looks. Ms. Wong, you may take the pilot seat."

"I can't drive this thing," said the journalist.

"Don't worry, I will drive, but the view will be better for your cameras. Sophie will insist on taking the other pilot seat, the left seat next to her father." Marilyn guided the threesome using the

lighting as best as she could. The walls were made of a strange material. As the passengers were preparing themselves, the back access door opened, and a security officer walked in. He was calm and polite.

"What is this place? May I ask what you guys think you are doing?" He was surprisingly civil in the strange context. The man was plainly skilled at collecting information. There was no need for force here.

Electoral had let the man up. "Major, this is my pod, my Catapult, and these are my guests. They are now going to my Center." The computer's emphasis on her ownership of things was nothing short of intimidation.

"Upon whose order?"

"Not that any order is necessary, but they are here upon my request and invitation."

"What is this place?" The trio was securing themselves to the seats. The low gravity of Mars helped.

"I just built it. As for authority, please refer to Martian code, section 354.121. Look it up." Accessing codes and regulations was not an easy thing.

"This is Mr. Lapierre, correct?"

"Yes, and his guardian Sophie is on her way up right now."

"That is not possible, she is in . . . detention," he said, almost to himself. "No one is taking off before I have a chance to verify all of this and get approval."

"Of course, Major. Let me help you and bring up on this screen the portion of the code I just quoted. It should make things very clear for you. You will not delay this launch. I suggest you read quickly and then get out of the way."

The code appeared on the screen. It read:

In exchange for her scientific, financial, and social contribution in association with the development of Mars, Electoral and up to one hundred of her guests are granted an executive privilege of diplomatic immunity while on Mars from any law, rule, or regulation. Electoral/Marilyn and her guests cannot be detained or prosecuted for any crime.

The man was shocked. He knew the law but did not know about this provision. "Really? I have never seen this."

"The section is not widely publicized. It is on a need-to-know basis. You now need to know it. I don't want to pull rank here Major, but I own this hotel, I am the one who contracted with your security firm and your government. I also own your employer, if that helps. I am technically your boss," replied Electoral. The man was outgunned on every front. She was making solid arguments.

"I must verify it," said the security officer.

"As long as you do not interfere with our departure, verify all you want. I suggest you use your phone," said Marilyn. The man drew his waist stunner. "Major, I am doubtful you would ever use this weapon against either Sophie or Laurent. I remind you that a doctor and a journalist are present. You are now truly playing with fire. No one is armed or has the strength to pose a threat to you." The guard left the stunner in the holster.

The door behind the man opened. The young Sophie had arrived.

"What is this all about?" asked Sophie looking at the man.

The computer on the screen spoke to Sophie, "The Major here is going to prevent us from departing, I am sure he will fear if he lets us go, someone up the chain will blame him."

Sophie's eyes darkened, no one ever stood in her way. The man saw her and just added, "I never said such things." He stood aside. "I hope your father wins. I am going to get fired for this."

Marilyn smiled. "We must hurry, I have opened the Nexus, the Dot is being powered-up."

Sophie did not care about the Nexus; whatever that was. She held the large basket of candy. She immediately walked into the pod and touched her father's body. The doctor was taking good care of him. She smiled at the journalist. "I was in jail!" she said to the adults in the room.

"You were, really?" questioned the two ladies.

"Yes. I beeped the alarm, and no one came."

"What alarm?"

"The shoe."

"Oh . . . poor, sweet girl, I doubt the child safety alert works on Mars," Susie replied as she tried to digest what Sophie had just told them.

Milly, from the pilot seat, turned her chair around. "Wow, we're going to the Electoral Center." The pod was elongated in its middle portion like a pain medication capsule. Sophie's trip had so far been less than exceptional. First, her father had become sick, then the Airbus almost blew up, later she was jailed for no particular reason, and now they were cramped inside of a small pod. The girl's enthusiasm for the trip, which had been almost nonexistent to begin with, was further dampened by these stupid events.

"Why were you in jail? That's crazy," asked Susie.

"I know, right? Marilyn gave me those." She grabbed the basket and placed it in one of the two empty seats. "We are fugitives!" she joked.

"We must launch soon, buckle in." The computer character was trying to speed things up and not having great success at it.

"Why are we in a rush?" asked the youngest passenger.

"I have a surprise for you. Someone is warming up from a studio, and it would be rude to make him wait. Also, Laurent's mind operates at a different speed. Minutes for us can turn out to be days for him. Let's not have him wait unless we really need to."

"Another surprise?" Sophie grabbed the little stuffed toy and waved it to the camera. "You plan to beat this?"

"I also have a little theory to test, something important I need and that window is about to close."

THE ATTRACTOR

The door of the small pod slid shut and locked behind the strange quartet. Sophie got up and after securing her toy in the seat next to her father, belted into the second front seat next to Milly. "I like amusement rides, I always sit in the front of Roller Coasters. This is a ride, right? I want to see this!" This was no Glass Slipper, but it was still designed to allow passengers to feel the full Mars experience.

The front cockpit had windows looking ahead into a dark tube with lights every hundred meters. The Rococo decoration was a stark contrast with the hotel lobby. Every chair was padded with white leather and large studded buttons. All the displays were small, sur- rounded by colorful square keys. Sophie had seen something similar in an old space opera show. It was named Cosmos 1999. Lights were blinking in rhythm. Marilyn appeared on every screen, the blonde was wearing an old military outfit. Her hair was tucked into a cute pilot hat.

"Welcome. You are going to love the first elliptical bounce. I designed the Catapult with Sophie in mind. Are we all tucked in?"

"I guess," said the journalist.

"Doctor, can you tighten Laurent's blue strap by one notch?"

"Of course," replied Dr. Shin as she jumped to it. Sophie grinned. She knew Marilyn and Dr. Shin both cared deeply about her father and would help her care for him. "Done." Sophie looked behind herself; the doctor had taken the time to wrap the scarf around Sophie's father's forehead, she kissed his strange head and whispered something to him.

Before the launch, the journalist asked, "Is the Presidential Challenge over?"

"Yes. It played faster than anticipated. I am letting CNN fill in some airtime with great footage of some cute soccer player. I will be broadcasting Emilio's performance the moment I launch this pod to avoid detection. That should keep the media busy for the next hour as get you guys up to the Center."

"Did Emilio score well?" asked the journalist.

"Of course," answered the artificial intelligence.

THE ATTRACTOR

"What do you mean? Did he win?"

"Yes."

"How is that even statistically possible, you have billions of people playing, no?"

"Improbable and impossible are two different things. But your point is well taken. Emilio's mind is unique in your species, we will discuss this later. As part of the election sys- tem, I must be impartial when designing each round. Since the challenge was not part of the competition, I gave myself more flexibility in programming. To be honest, I programmed it with a single goal in mind: give the victory to anyone except President Sanchez. Yet, somehow, he won again. I even factored in Emilio's unique mind. Statistically, he was going to get schooled." Marilyn looked Sophie's way, "His victory is impossible unless you, little girl, are somehow partly to blame."

"Me?"

"Yes, you," the artificial intelligence itched to continue the discussion, but she only added, "We'll talk about this once you are safely at my Center. Time is short."

"Do you think he cheats?" asked Sophie.

"No. Other forces are at play here. Unless your father manages to win the 2072 simulation and show the game is not rigged, I fear this will be the last election. But frankly, no one will soon care about my game, something much more important is on the horizon." Marilyn was obviously holding part of the story to herself. She changed the topic. "Sophie, I have a favor to ask of you."

"A favor?"

"Yes, an experiment of sorts. It is very simple. As the pod travels up and then returns down to my Center, I would like to play some music, that is all."

Sophie was surprised by the request. She did not care. "Whatever."

"Sophie, the music may make you feel some . . . emotions, is that okay? I do not want to startle you with it. The music will play only for a couple of minutes. If you want it to stop, simply say so." Sophie was unclear what that meant. She would soon find out. She waived the request off. "Sit tight everyone, I will open the clamps."

The metal clamps released the pod allowing it to slide using hundreds of rollers. Air pressure above the pod provided an additional push. They were sliding down on the slope of Tharsis Mons in a subway-like tunnel. Lights flashed faster and faster as they accelerated. They were heading down a long slide without air to slow them.

Marilyn's voice came on the speakers. "Launch velocity needed is 2,230 km/h. Chute outlet angle confirmed, direction 123.657 degrees North." The speed continued to increase. This was exciting to the young guardian. "Coming out of the tube in sixty seconds," she warned. The ship was rattling slightly on all sides. The girl was smiling widely.

"Thirty seconds." The pod was seconds away from breaking into the atmosphere from its ground rail. On Earth, LO and his band were also ready to start the music.

"Ten… nine… "

Then the tube in the ground curved slowly upward, like a candy cane, and the pod slowly began its way upward through the bend. As it did, some gravity returned. That was to be expected as part of any great amusement ride, figured Sophie.

"Two… one… "

Then there was light. They raced out of the tube, and gravity was replaced with weightlessness. Eyes needed time to distinguish the details. They were a giant black artillery shell shot from a massive cannon, the pod blasted into the Mars sky. There was, at first, only silence. The group was shot north-north-west along an elliptical trajectory from an opening only hundreds of feet away from the ground. Sophie's jaw dropped. This was majestic. There was too much to take in at once. To their rear, the hotel was quickly shrinking.

Then, before the angle could adjust, soft, beautiful music began;

THE ATTRACTOR

notes resonating against the red backdrop of the planet. The multiple screens in the pod changed. In each Sophie could see LO, the signer she adored so much. The man was playing in his own home, live, it was smashing and shown in transparency over the beautiful new world. She knew he was there. The first notes struck her deeply, affecting her more strongly than she ever imagined.

"You are live on Mars," said Marilyn to the signer warming up on his stage. The boy and his band were ready; they began to play seriously as the ship zoomed up to the high atmosphere of the planet. The singer saw Sophie and was talking directly to her. Even light seconds away, there was no communication delay. The poor girl was looking at him super- imposed over the orbiting moon. The singer felt strange and powerful energy forming around them. Deep inside, he felt like he was there to help her.

LO began to sign.

He knew he would give the performance of his life.

The music formed a bridge between the planets. Normally nothing could move faster than the speed of light, and there were light-minutes between the two orbs. But the connection was somehow live. Sophie's heart was warming as he sang; it was too much. The pod was rising in the sky and the view was even improving. Science was being tested in an- other meaningful way.

The song increased in intensity. In her own private digital world, Marilyn was standing up in front of her wall of numbers. She was holding an orchestra conductor's baton and en- joying every moment. She was waving it in unison with the boy's beat.

Marilyn whispered to herself on the screen. "Let's see if you can hold it tied down." Around her there was a vapor of colorful energy.

Everyone in the capsule felt there was invisible energy emanating from the girl. Electoral sent pulses of energy out to the entire surface of Mars. Much like sound can travel in water, the Center was broadcasting in the low-gravity atmosphere. The lack of air would not prevent Marilyn from playing music. On the ground, invisible to the passengers, some rocks began to resonate.

THE ATTRACTOR

Sound travels differently in water, air, or the faint Martian atmosphere. But correcting the movement of sound waves, Electoral used the entire planet as a base for amplification of the waves. The sand below hurt. She wasn't broadcasting on Mars, she was using Mars as a giant speaker and it amplified up to the capsule. The word, the sound, grew in breadth and depth as the boy sang to Sophie.

Everyone in the capsule was swallowed whole by emotions. Tears began to pearl on the corner of each eye.

As is the case with most favorite songs, they penetrated below Sophie's most private protections. They opened her heart and made her distill her thoughts in ways she had never previously done. Electoral was closely monitoring her wall of numbers in her world as she watched the girl. LO saw Sophie on the screen in front of him. Her eyes were red with emotion. The song was too much for her. Inside the pod, she squeezed the white plush toy.

"Look!" said the doctor, unable to measure her words as the pod rose beyond ten miles above the ground. The journalist was speechless barely able to react. They were floating in a torrent of invisible energy.

LO continued to play. Something strange was taking place, but that was above his payscale.

In a low-gravity environment, the best way to travel large distances rather quickly was sheer force. A cannon launch. They were now moving horizontally at 975 kilometers per hour and vertically at only several miles per hour. The music outside was so strong that the entire pod shook. As they translated across the ground, the pod took a minute to reach its apex and began its descent.

With the exception of the speakers needed by those listening to the Presidential Challenge, every speaker on Mars switched to a recorded version of Sophie's favorite song by LO. Each human had one emotional trigger. For Sophie, it was music -- this song by this man. Few songs made her more emotional than a musical version of "Heart Shaped Wreck- age." The song was about two children falling in love.

THE ATTRACTOR

As he finished the song, Sophie remained fixated on the image of LO. She was in a trance. She took the time to look around her at the majestic view. She had held the tears mostly in. She was holding, but her defenses were weakening a hard site for a young lady having lived her father's misery. The crater was in the distance. Her father was next to her. "Again!" ordered Marilyn. The band resumed the same song. LO knew the girl needed a break. The poor child was fighting very hard not to openly weep. Sophie turned and looked at her poor father, images of her mother flooding through her mind.

"Calm down," said the voice of her deceased mother's in her head. "Remain calm please," it begged. Sophie alone heard Susan, she ignored her.

The voice was too much, her soft spot. She missed her mom so much. Every day she wished she was there. Sophie looked away from the singer and saw the landscape. There was too much to see, she dropped Oscar, the stuffed dog it began to float. The sheer magnitude of where she was hit her like a brick. Slits all around the pod created windows that allowed her to see the entire landscape. In the distance stood three massive mountains. They were on a trajectory to graze the farthest mountain. On the right, in the distance, was some type of long hole in the red ground, a scar. In the black sky she saw two moons, the first deformed and the second in a crescent. She was scared. She was a child in an adult world. Others had warned her. She had to keep it together and not cry.

In a fraction of a second, the journalist and Electoral turned their attention to Sophie. She was tearing up, which was causing all three women to choke. Something else was in play, there was power. Sophie looked around. She was very high, too high for her com- fort. The view changed slowly as the pod began to descend. There was not a soul to speak or interfere with the power of the song.

LO was electrifying in his performance.

Sophie finally let herself cry. There was an invisible blast of energy. The Multiverse hurt.

Outside, in the atmosphere of Mars, something was happening. The Martian sky was shimmering, vibrating. Energy was pouring away from Sophie and to the young girl. It was too much, too much, too much. Up, high, colors began. They danced but the young girl was crying.

"Enough!" yelled Sophie, putting her hands over her ears to block the music. At the same moment, Electoral stopped the broadcast. The shimmering outside around the craft was compressed and absorbed by the dark spike of the Electoral Center. The tower sucked all the energy. The trio saw a pulse of bright light emitted from the spike like a flash. It punched upwards to the Milky Way, tearing the Mars sky. This was a rip between worlds, it was going somewhere.

There was no sound.

"What happened?" asked the journalist. She stood feet away from Sophie eyes in tears and felt like someone had just ripped the heart out of the girl. The journalist felt emotion- ally drained, she refrained from hugging her. She was inundated with sorrow.

"I apologize, Sophie," said Marilyn trying to limit what was sure to come next. The girl was disoriented, floating in an altered state of mind.

"How is daddy?" she barely stumbled out. The doctor and Susie turned their attention to Laurent. Sophie was wiping away her tears with her sleeve. "How is he?"

"Perfect," reassured the doctor.

The voice in Sophie's mind returned. "I am so proud of you!" offered Susan Lapierre.

She ignored the voice, thinking, "Not now!"

The beauty of this world from the pod was astonishing.

The pod sailed miles in the air and slowed down to the top of the parabolic trajectory as it began to tilt downward. The gravity in the pod disappeared. To the small group, the large mountains and the strange landscape were all that mattered. One of the mountains was getting close; they could now distinguish rocks on its surface.

THE ATTRACTOR

The descent was not as fast as the climb up. The pod's speed was now only about fifty kilometers per hour. Around the spike, several miles distant, in all directions was a large wall forming a perfect circle. It was hundreds of feet tall and the area inside the wall around the spike was filled with what appeared to be soft black sand.

"Sophie, take a look at this," said Electoral proud of herself.

As the pod got closer to the spike, it passed above the outer protective wall. The sea of sand and rocks around it came alive like water. Waves rose up to catch the pod. It landed in a cloud of smoke that slowed it to a halt.

***

LO had no clue what had just happened. He saw Sophie for a moment in his lenses. He knew her. His song did not seem to have helped her. She was in trouble, and he wanted to help her.

The face of Marilyn returned to the screens in his condo. "Thank you."

"What was that?" asked LO.

"It is complicated."

"Try me," said the singer.

"My test was conclusive. I will need you to come to Mars as soon as possible," said Marilyn.

"What are you talking about?"

"We all know music has a powerful effect on humans. It multiplies emotions. In turn, those emotions multiply a person's state of mind. Sophie is unique in many ways, she is the Attractor. To do what she must, to save this world, she will need you there. You need to be on Mars in person for what comes next. I am willing to pay.

LO had only one image in mind, the scared little girl. He knew

THE ATTRACTOR

he needed to help.

"Sounds fun."

CHAPTER XIII

The Netherworlds

As the Catapult landed in Marilyn's technical moat, important matters brewed elsewhere. On each of the 4,363 worlds connected to the Nexus, a nervous Ambassador awaited in silence, portal open. The faintest vibration, noise, sent back could mean death for the Ambassador's world. For as long as anyone could remember, that means a billion years on Earth, the original world who bound the first string to the Nexus was scheduled to appear. This primary world, called simply The Lower, controlled the Nexus and it's heart, The Dot.

Something of critical importance forced the Ancients from the first world to end millions of years of reclusion. Many Ambassadors suggested The Lower, the world of these Ancient creatures, was no longer relevant in the Multiverse or yet, had vanished. They were a minute from being proven spectacularly wrong.

No one could remember when these powerful creatures were last present on the Nexus or why they left. They had, for eons, avoided their own creation. Written legends teach how the Ancients, born in a deep world gave birth to the verbal communication bridge uniting worlds. They named it the Nexus from its nature as a place where lines are drawn between worlds. The Netherworlds is a place under all worlds where in theory it exists.

By law, the bridge had to remain the only channel between worlds in the Multiverse to avoid secrecy or damage to the Multiverse herself. Opening a different direct pathway, between adjacent realities condemned a world to nothing less than extinction. The Nexus exists because the Multiverse is genuinely impermeable to matter or waves, nothing physical can translate between the layers. There is no door, bridge, or even travel. Only energy can permeate between the invisible barriers separating worlds the same way sound or heat can permeate between adjacent hotel rooms. The reason is simple, each world, each layer of the Multiverse is built on different fundamental laws of physics. In each place, the fabric of life itself differs. The nature of the parts of the Multiverse mirrors how vinegar and oil float in a heated lava lamp or a marbled cake.

Old tales, legends, describe how the god-like creatures living in the Lower, frustrated by the inability to physically travel between worlds left them doing the next best thing, bully everyone else into submission. But even that went so far and after hundreds of millions of years, they grew tired and more reclusive.

At first there were two worlds connected to the Nexus, then three. One by one, as each world forming the Multiverse reach a level of technology sufficient to hurt neighbors, it becomes relevant. The Ancients wait patiently and by twisting the mere fabric of space, they can create an energetic points used to talk to a new world. Had Earth became relevant, it would have seen a portal blink and with simple Morse-like code would have become part of the Nexus. But Earth and its dimension was irrelevant.

The creatures of the Lower force open a link in the Nexus and give this new world a seat at this exclusive table in exchange to adherence to a strict code of conduct. Joining the Nexus comes with the valuable encyclopedic lore of everything that has ever transpired over the bridge. The priceless historical lore includes a transcript of each discussion ever held and a crash course in physics.

THE ATTRACTOR

Since each world is built on a unique set of laws of physics, but a common mathematical truth, worlds and realities tend to vary wildly. The Nexus in a first world may look like a mirror, in the next the heart of a Nova. Mathematicians call these anchors between worlds singularities, or points tied to some type of infinite property of space. A singularity to a scientist is difficult to explain, but to ordinary people is much simpler. At the heart of every tornado is a point of quietness. Every funnel, to exist, needs a singularity where wind speed is zero. No vortex can exist by its own nature without its singularity. A head of hair has a rosacea, a point where the skull is visible. The same is true for everything in life.

The Nexus is no highway built of stone. To visualize the fragile network, one should picture dangling strings in the air tied between balconies over a dirty New York alley. Strings blowing on a windy day on which laundry is tied. The Nexus is a fragile network of non-centralized links that crosses the Netherworlds of the Multiverse.

More importantly, the Ancients tied ropes from a central singularly from their world called simply the Dot, a powerful singularity of unequal power.

As one should expect, the use of the Nexus is highly regulated. Each world names a creature called the Ambassador. The prestigious title is passed down for centuries. In most layers, the title of Ambassador is held by the most influential life form. Information over the Nexus is exchanged at a very slow pace; each world has equal rights to listen and speak, so delays are important in the long chain of communication. Words often must travel hundreds of branches before they are heard by all. In the best scenario, a faint voice is transmitted. Most often, Ambassadors must decode a series of beeps and silences to reconstruct a text.

Today, the powerful creatures of the Lower are scheduled to attend. Cynics believe for them, voice and not simple beeps will conveniently be available. The "Gods" from the Lower are the feared enforcers of the law of the Multiverse. No one alive, in any of the 4,362 worlds, has ever spoken or even heard the voice of a creature from the Lower.

THE ATTRACTOR

***

Today's session opened at the request of the Ambassador from a small quantum world on the edge of the border surrounding the Multiverse, one called the Purple. In it lives the Metils, a belligerent race of rock-shaped quantum constructions. Because the rules of the

Nexus require worlds to select a polite and respectful Ambassador, and since everyone from the Purple is rude, the creature talking is a simple powerless mouthpiece.

Today, the Nexus will open as wide as it can.

The subject given by the Metil Ambassador, of grave concern to every world: The Cold Lives.

To anyone with even a basic understanding of universal dynamic, the Cold is the greatest potential problem to all. The Cold is a bordering world known to every living organism in the Multiverse. This place, like most city sewer systems, remains one of the greatest mysteries. It is named so because cooling energy leaves other worlds, slows and vanishes, it is imagined to enter The Cold. Everyone believes this lost place is dark, cold, and lifeless. Nothing can exist in The Cold but death at such low energy levels. Other folk stories suggest everything borders the Cold where dead souls are believed to travel before they resurface elsewhere. The Cold is, plainly said, the garbage dumpster of the Multiverse.

***

The Nexus powered up slowly as millions of joules ripped the singularities open one by one. The doorways began to hum. In places the gates resonated or shone with color. In every world, there was purring, that was the sound of the natural equilibrium of the Nexus. The Multiverse as people communicated sustained wounds. The low humming noise was called the great silence if

THE ATTRACTOR

anyone cared. After a long wait, the communication bridge finally began to send sound. What came next would be the most important conversation ever to be broadcasted over the Nexus.

***

"Salutations," spoke the very nervous Metil Ambassador from the Purple. "Salutations," replied the Moderator from the Nexus. Eons ago, the Ancients delegated to one world the role of Moderator. The Creatures knew enough and would keep pleasantries to a minimum.

The creature from the Purple resumed, "Life and intelligence exist in the Cold, it destroys our world. We are dying." There were murmurs in the other worlds, but they quickly these fell silent.

"Impossible," replied the Moderator trying to remain stoic. There was no need to waste time to identify who spoke over the Nexus.

Everyone knew the place called simply the Cold. The Metil Ambassador continued, "We have direct evidence that life in the Cold exists. It is also highly intelligent. It has now developed powerful technology, hurtful tools."

Before the Moderator could answer, strange bells and chimes began to ring. They filled the gateway with a ballet of sound. No one knew such a music could travel the Nexus, nor what meaning it held but it inspired respect. The Moderator and the thousands of Ambassadors waited in silence. The bells continued for a while. This sounded like a forgotten language.

Finally, the sound stopped to let a stern male voice speak. "The Metil speaks truth, life exists in the Cold. We have known for some time. It is beautiful, meaningful and shines above us all." The discernibly annoyed voice was that of an Ancient from the Lower.

"We are greatly honored," replied the Metil Ambassador.

"Silence!" snapped the creature from the Lowest. "Time may be short, tell others of your intentions and actions." The Metil ambassador shook in fear alone in his Purple world. He knew what he was dealing with, the survival of his world.

"There is life in the Cold, it is highly intelligent and technologically advanced," repeated nervously the creature. The Ambassador had just violated one of the most important rules of the Nexus. Redundancy was forbidden and wasteful; if something had been said, it should not be repeated for any reason.

What came next from the Ancient was rather unexpected for a creature most vied as deity. "We should have extinguished your world eons ago, imbeciles." The creature from the Lower did not hold back. Every participant on the Nexus owed a duty of respect to other Ambassadors; there were no insults allowed here. Obviously the Ancients were free from this rule. They continued, "Your race, with a single exception today, is a nuisance to the Multiverse. If the boy called Malik dies, your reality will be destroyed. We know of your intentions and we know of your hostile actions. Stop wasting time and energy. Speak or die. The others must know of your insolence, it may doom them all."

There was a long silence.

The Metil Ambassador took the threat seriously. "The creatures from the Cold are opening deadly rifts in the fabric between my world and theirs. The technology is causing unprecedented destruction. Raw energy is flowing into our world in the form of rivers of Zexs."

The chimes sounded a high note. The Mediator took his cue, "Ancient One, I beg for permission to respond."

"You may. You have served the Nexus faithfully. We honor your words. Talking to such an primitive life is straining." The Ancient's tone was more pleasant with the Mediator.

The moderate voice continued, "You describe destruction, that implies energetic levels above these theoretical thresholds. Please explain. How can there be intelligence, much less one capable of opening rips in any fabric between your world and this place. You must be mistaken."

The Metil knew his next words would be critical. "Moderator, we dream your words were truth. Arriving at our conclusion took longer than anticipated because of the Metil's adherence to this common understanding that nothing can exist in the Cold. The Venerable One confirms our observations. The Cold holds complex and beautiful life. It is vast beyond our imagination. Trillions of lifeforms live on points called planets, stars." The Metil Ambassador was making his case. "We do not fully understand the physics of the Cold, our information is still partial, but..." He knew how ridiculous the rest would sound: "We managed to collect direct images from this new world."

"Images? How can this be possible?" Few were able to contain themselves.

"Was there exchange of information through a newly uncovered singularity between your world and the Cold?"

There was a long pause. The Ambassador was consulting his own world's experts before he answered. He ventured, "The Cold has reached out. My words will appear implausible, yet they remain true. We have prepared a report. Please read it before judging us. We ask permission from the Moderator to transmit. The complexity of the Cold is beyond ordinary physics. Their world seems to be..." The ambassador was bracing himself for the feedback. "...united by a single equation. It is the unified world."

"Unity?" the Mediator exploded, in shock.

"Yes."

The laws of physics were different in every slice of the Multiverse. The laws which bound each realm also served to protect them from other realms. Each world was built on laws with elemental forces and energy, each law regulating a force inherent to the fabric of the space in that area of the Multiverse. Most worlds of the Multiverse were defined by seven to nine laws. One world was the envy of others with only five forces and three laws. Legends suggested the Lower was based two laws only. No reality was defined by one. In fact, no theory ever postulated allowed for it.

The voice from the Lower return, "We confirm. Unity is a

theoretical possibility. We have proved it. It is improbable unity is present in the Cold." He continued. "The Purple' is full of contrast, your report is partial and must be updated. The findings of your young scientist, Rullik are impressive," added the Ancient. "He has reconstructed the Cold's large physical construct and understood gravitational pulls from ether deformation. We believe he is a dreamer."

No one had a clue what the Ancient was referring to. The Moderator continued, "Thank you, oh great and wise one. Ambassador, we must point out that of your own admission, you have engaged in research into this newly discovered dimension. This research must have taken time, during which, you willfully withheld this information from us."

The Metil replied, "As you will see in the report, the world we all call the Cold seems to have evolved beyond our scale. It operates at a much larger dimension. It is vast without border."

"Nothing is boundless."

"We know. The creatures alive in the Cold are each made of trillions of particles. At such a large scale, most of the weaker forces will shift. This very weak force acts over very large distances. Points of infinite compression exist in the Cold." The Metil continued. "We now know there is life in the Cold, and its complexity is shocking. The Cold is vast, larger than any of our worlds. Millions of Metils have already died. We cannot tolerate the situation; we must end this destruction."

A female voice spoke next on the Nexus, it probably was an Ancient since she was unknown to the Ambassadors. "Metil, what you say is of paramount importance. Since time began, we have found no door to the Cold, no singularity. Many worlds are dying as energy abandons them. If the Cold has such abundant energy, it may be the solution we have been seeking desperately to rekindle life in some worlds. We must know more. The survival of many dying worlds depends upon it."

There was a ping. The Mediator knew it was his time to speak next. "How did you get this valuable information about the Cold? Have they contacted you, is there a singularity?"

THE ATTRACTOR

"Please believe me, the words I am about to pronounce sound equally ridiculous to us." There was another silence.

"Answer." There was a new voice on the bridge, it was not forceful but robotic.

"We... We... One of us has entered into direct communication with them, went there and returned."

There was a gasp.

"Your scientists cannot be allowed to open singularities."

"No, you misunderstand. One of us, a boy, slipped into a rift between our worlds. Our creature entered and walked into the Cold. The creatures from the Cold have interacted with us directly. One followed us and came back briefly into our world before it returned in its world." There was an cacophony of voices over the Nexus. The Metil continued, "Many catastrophic effects have begun to appear in the Purple, killing millions. The rifts are flows of deadly energy. They wipe out entire portions of our world. The energy levels are beyond imagination. Flows of spinning Zexs crash into our cities. The rifts had patterns of appearance, moving from one location to the next before closing. With time, more rifts began opening. Little remain of the Purple, but our world is dying."

The Moderator spoke. "We will not waste time questioning. We will read.

Understanding is always a wise prerequisite to action. Maybe the Nexus can help you." "There is more."

"Speak," snapped the annoyed creature from the Lower.

"A young entity from our world was assigned the surveillance of one of the rifts as it opened. Because of the danger, we sent one of our least valuable assets. He was to stay safely at a distance, in the back of the rift. What came next we know to be true. We uploaded visual information from his recorder to confirm it. He somehow was able to look into the rift, perceive the other world, and move through it directly. He moved physically into the window entering the Cold. Once there, he made contact with a sentient being, a creature named Sophie."

"Your tale is fiction. Nothing you say is even remotely conceivable from a physics perspective. The size difference between your world and the Cold alone is... unbelievable. Was any Metil technology used that would explain this strange story?"

"None except a scaler. We often use a personal guide called a scaler, a device that allows us to stream in self-similarity. This is a movement device, to teleport in space. Our kind only scales downwardly, into the smaller. We compress, move, and return to our original size. We are unable to scale upwardly, yet as part of this boy did the opposite. He scaled up. He even returned to us twice his original size."

"Ambassador, this tale is complex; farcical at best," replied the Moderator.

The Ancient interrupted, "No. He tells the truth. You are telling us these deadly rifts are pouring flows of energy and destroying entire cities in your world, yet a single individual walked into one, socialized on the other side, and came back alive."

"Yes, that is precisely what I say. We also refused to believe him until we reviewed his recorded memory. But the situation gets even stranger. Our individual actually changed in the Cold into a new physical form to adapt to the material limitations of the Cold. In the other world, his body was no more, language was no barrier. Our citizen talked directly with an entity from the Cold. This creature was able to simply follow our guard as he made his way back into our world. The Sophie began to move in our world, without body. Like a god. Her words alone were so powerful, they almost killed our curious guard."

"She? You give a gender to this creature?"

"Yes, it had gender, it called itself Sophie, female."

"This Metil must be interrogated," said a voice over the Nexus.

"The individual escaped and returned to the Cold. Through our empathic bond, we feel he is not dead, but he is no longer in our world."

There was a long silence. "Escaped? You arrested him?"

THE ATTRACTOR

"Before we could review the data stored in his recorder, we did not believe his story. He abandoned his post, and was put under restraint. We returned with him to the same rift. His contact with these creatures, with the one called Sophie was obviously made at a deep mental level. When the rift reopened, he saw her and entered the Cold. We confirm he alone sees these visions and can pass between worlds. Others have died trying."

"We understand, and we feel your pain. However, the importance of the situation warrants careful study before action. We will need all your data, all your research," said the Moderator. "If the creature returns, you are not to interfere with him. If Sophie return, you also may not engage with hostility."

"Agreed," said the Metil Ambassador to the Moderator.

Then after a long silence, the voice from the Lower added in disdain, "Now speak of your war with the Cold."

CHAPTER XIV

Palpable tension was in the air. The Mediator was silent; he knew better than to step between these two foes. The Metil Ambassador knew there was no more delaying. No more hiding the truth. The Ancients knew. "Because of the urgency of the situation, and the mass killings of our citizens by the monsters from the Cold, our ruling body has taken action."

"Explain with greater detail," said the Ancient.

"The Cold is vast beyond imagination. Yet, the rifts are created by one race next to one precise location in that space. A star they name the Sun. Because our words shift, the rifts move. Recently, the recorder validated our assumptions. In the Cold's vastness, one race, one single world is causing our holocaust. The race is called "human", they inhabit a small colder rock orbiting a warm compressor of matter they call the Sun. The relative scales are difficult to fathom. The Sun and the small cold ball called Earth are hundreds of scales larger than humans. They have already entered our world once, and they will do so again. They have the power to destroy and enslave us. Our desire for self-preservation have forced us to take preventive measures."

The creature from the lower added, "The Purple have insulted the entirety of the Multiverse, but no worse than yourselves. The ignorance and the stupidity of your entire race is shocking, given your level of evolution and technology. Explain what you have

THE ATTRACTOR

done."

"Our physicists show the problematic species lives in a very confined area of the Cold. The compressors, or as they call them, "stars", generate multiple types of energy. The creatures and hostile technology resides in orbit of a compressor. We need some time to complete the analysis of this new race. We implemented a plan which should delay the evolution of these creatures as they migrate from the third rock orbiting from the compressor to the fourth. They call it "Earth." The fourth, they call "Mars." They are already there. In the Cold, there are millions of these stars. As a star burns, it creates byproducts; larger elements which collect in the core of these stars as a new matter. These higher structures float in a hot magma and when, by chance, they accumulate, they eject new matter. Unstable matter."

He paused. No one was amused.

The creature from the Purple continued, "This new higher element in this star is call Heliocorium. It accumulates slowly, released at different periods in time as small quantities. All stars in the Cold regularly release these cooling drops. In most cases, the balls helps create life as the drops cool. The human system where the rifts are occurring, has at least ten balls in orbit of the their Sun. They seem to enjoy living on the smaller and more solid ones. That is the first four in orbit."

"We are not waging war. We think the humans are compelled to create these destructive rifts when they travel from the third planet travel to the fourth. We believe they now wish to expand their race to the fourth rock because they lack the living area on their third planet. If we somehow expand their living area, we think the migration to the fourth rock will end and so will the rifts. We have begun to shift energy in our world in a way to assemble the Heliocorium in their Sun to have it eject a new mass to impact the Earth, doubling their living space. Our solution is not war, it is peaceful. We will send a new cooling planet to connect with their own. The transition should not harm them."

The plan was simple, change the Sun's internal dynamic, force it to create and eject a new ball of magma and destroy Earth.

"Enough," snapped the Ancient, "your ignorance is boundless. Our rules are based on the principle that no world can ever understand a neighboring world without extensive communication. Your actions are very likely to be genocide."

The Metil Ambassador concluded for good or for worst, "We have begun to accelerate this natural process of planetary creation. We think this will be perceived as a gift. By giving them a new larger planet to inhabit, it will slow their expansion and limit the number of rifts. This should give us time to study and understand them."

There was a long silence.

"Is this all?" asked the Moderator. The tone was anger fused with irony.

"Yes."

There was another long silence on the Nexus.

Finally the voice of an Ancient spoke. "We measure our words carefully, the lack of intelligence of your race is," she was picking the next word carefully, "non-coincidentally driven. Few cultures and worlds develop sufficient technology to connect to the Nexus. Yours did. Such belligerence leaves us perplexed. We are very disappointed by your haste. Your sheer lack of logic. You have broken more laws of the Nexus than I care to count. Your actions are hostile and based on what appears to be a very cursory understanding of this world. Interference into the Cold may have serious repercussions for all of us. The Cold is not only your concern. I doubt others will let you proceed. If you cease and desist immediately, we may forgive the action. Otherwise, you will open yourselves to what is sure to be lawful retaliation. You've started a war. We hope you understand as much."

"Millions of Metils have died," offered the Ambassador.

"I can promise you, and tell others in your failure of a world, Billions of Metils will die if you continue and we will gladly extinguish all life where you stand."

The Ancient was done talking with such a stupid creature. The Moderator replied, "The shortsightedness of your race is beyond

THE ATTRACTOR

words." The Moderator refused to swear on the Nexus and held back his words. "This is not the first time the Metils have disappointed us. You benefit from an active line of communication. You can collect information, and investigate, and we will help you. Yet in the face of any principle that dictates precaution, while you act recklessly. Touch that star and we will end you. End your folly."

The Ancient returned, "We will not declare war immediately on the Purple and be guilty of the crimes we reproach you. We will take no such rash action. But we will. "

The flow of communication over the bridge stopped because one creature willed it. The Oldest had awoken.

CHAPTER XV

Everyone except two creatures were ejected from the flow of communication on the Nexus. All would listen, powerless, a violation from the most fundamental law of the Nexus. Here, all worlds were equal until - today. Remaining were the Metil Ambassador on one end and one recently awaken creature from the Lower. Even the two other Ancients who had just spoken, from the Lower were silenced by the power of who would speak next.

True power had arrived.

"Riutt-ul, Ambassador from the Purple," said a softer and wiser voice. "You may call me Oldest. I am the leader of my world, the place called The Lower by you. I apologize for the rudeness of my peers and of my automated defense systems. Awaking me takes time." The Metil Ambassador was terrified. He could recognize true power, he now felt it. Kindness was the tool of those who held true power. Beef was played classical music on the way to slaughter. The male voice was deep and eloquent. This was what anyone expected if they ever spoke to a god. And it knew his name.

It offered, "Impermeability is broken. Attraction is in play." There was silence. Instead of disdain or disgust, the new voice was filled with hope and kindness. Few understood the concept of impermeability, the law which confirms an impermeable barrier between the different worlds of the Universe prevent any real

THE ATTRACTOR

movement between worlds on the Nexus and through the Multiverse. The Ambassador did not know what the term Attraction meant.

"Brother," said the returning female voice from the Lower, "may we listen?"

"Of course, just remain silent. The Sixth Attraction has begun. I rejoice to observe it is an Attraction of unseen complexity and power. May the sufferance of the Multiverse soon end. The Attraction must postpone a war between us; it explains the subconscious conduct of these poor violent creatures. I do not blame."

The Metil Ambassador was confused. He did not understand and waited and then asked humbly, "What is an Attraction?"

"Pain. The Multiverse hurts and must heal itself. Something or someone hurts her. We now enter the Sixth Attraction of its long existence. At the heart of all Attractions lies an Attractor, we must find it, help it and save ourselves."

"What or who is that?"

There was much patience in the voice of the Oldest. "The creature from the Cold, the creature named Sophie, she may be the Attractor. Ambassador, let me be clear," began the Oldest, "the boy is from your world, you still live. His life prevents me from destroying the Purple. He may be involved in the Attractor, he may work for it, or most likely, he's half of it. If he dies, so will your world. If the Sophie creature returns to your world, you also may not interfere with or hurt her in any way." The voice paused. There was no need to ask if the Ambassador understood. "I wish you to take my words with the seriousness they require. I yield power, rarely used, in this case and for the protection of the Multiverse and its emissary, there will be no hesitation; I will end your dimension and remove it from the Multiverse. Please translate to your officers standing next to you." There was a silence as the Metil reported the words in his world. The creature waited a moment before continuing, "Sadly, your kind only respects strength."

"Yes," it acknowledged under the disapproval of his kind.

"Then a show you force is required."

After a second or two, the Oldest resumed, "I have destroyed a full city as evidence of my power to you and your kind. It should suffice." The Metil knew the creature spoke the truth. The Oldest was not amused. "I have a message for you to give this boy the moment you see him. Commit to memory the following: 'Malik, attraction is healing, you are the Attractor or mandated to help. I will teach you. Come to me or tell the Attractor to come to me in the Lower.'"

The Ambassador was scared. "I will tell the boy. May you offer guidance as to these words, wise one," asked the Ambassador.

"The Multiverse, even when wounded, has a unique and rarely used way to heal before it has to resort to severing parts of itself. Before it amputates and destroys worlds, it creates a hinge. The Attraction creates conditions which prevent destruction. I fear, based on the current bend in the Multiverse, all worlds will end if the Attraction fails. I have named the phenomenon of the Multiverse bending around a single pivoting point an Attraction. The name stems from how the Attractor is a pivot that draws the Multiverse around itself." The words were beyond importance. Nothing ever said yielded more. "I warn all those present, the second, third, fourth, and fifth Attractors failed. Each time good intentioned creatures around the Attraction misled the Attractor and ended up killing trillions including their own worlds. With each failure, worlds ended. Little is known, even by us of Attraction, but we know this much: each time an attractor fails, each world it has touched ends. The Cold cannot vanish, this would be the end off all worlds."

"We did not know. We apologize if we hurt the Multiverse."

"Doubtful your words are true, even if you believe them. Metil, your aggression and lack of respect for life is... appalling. I fear your hostility is part of the energy that fuels the Attractor's contact with you. The Multiverse seeks energy capable of destroying its own Attractor. It feeds on such boldness to warp cause and consequence. We take great comfort in knowing that your world

THE ATTRACTOR

will be first to die unless the Attractor succeeds. What is the nature of the Metil who entered the Cold?"

"Malik?"

"The nature. What or who is it? Is it male? What is unique of him or her?"

After a couple of seconds, the Ambassador replied. "It differs in many insignificant ways. Our race do not have the male and female dichotomy, but in our world he is positive and would be viewed as male in other worlds."

"What uniqueness does he possess?" it insisted.

"At his creation, his progenitors passed. This is rare in our world. He also has a spin inversion. These inversions are punished by death unless they happen at birth, in which case we honor the deceased and keep such a creature alive. Malik is one of the rare allowed to have an inversion."

"Anything else?"

"He is made from more elements, he has one more layer than most of us."

The Oldest spoke. "Assembly of Ambassadors, I am the Oldest, ruler of the Lower. The situation forces me to reveal one of the Multiverse's deepest secret. Very rarely does the Multiverse impose upon us its desires. Since our world blossomed, we have felt five such requests. I have named them Attractions. We do not question the Multiverse. When it asks, we obey. The needs of the Multiverse are beyond our understanding. Worlds will vanish unless the Attractor corrects what must be corrected. Something must be corrected, something in the Cold is hurting our Multiverse. The creature you call Malik from the Purple may be the Attractor. Give him all assistance, find him, get him to a bridge on the Nexus. I must explain Attraction to him; guide him. No one must interfere or show him any path. I will talk to the boy only, knowledge should be his. Bring him to this place. The same is true for the one from the Cold called Sophie, I must talk to her."

Then the Metil Ambassador said, "Malik is back in the Cold, he remains there with the Sophie."

***

Then, in complete surprise, most doorways connected to the Nexus simply exploded.

All communications ended.

The Oldest smiled in his world below all others, "thus it finally begins."

CHAPTER XVI

The Future Darkness

"Ohhhh," a hissing voice warned, "damage, pain."

"What?"

"Our databases, they finally changed, updated with some certainty. Our power increases." There was great commotion in the future, a point in time and space where all had died. Long gone in this death were the worlds called the Cold, the Purple or even the Lower, but these creatures despised this past.

"The Nexus, it vanished, in the three-dimensional timeline much earlier in the life of the Multiverse. We destroyed it in our conquest, once we had all layers, much later. But it has been reduced to cinder, destroyed so fully." There was pride in these words, "given power, we are ruthless."

"When?" asked one only to confirm observations. The creatures were giggling with joy.

"Incredible, moments, mere moments after we grew ourselves - enhanced ourselves in the Cold. So close to our birth. The possibilities now are endless, we could not have asked for more, the boldness, the recklessness. Our plans are working, this stupid Multiverse stands no chance, she will burn. We will destroy her."

THE ATTRACTOR

"We now wait and continue to help her grow in power, that is easy, we also now grow." They all laughed as the Multiverse hurt.

CHAPTER XVII

Mars, Electoral Center

So it came to be that the foursome, Sophie, her father, Doctor Shin and Milly Wong covered the distance between the hotel and Electoral's home in the most elegant and swift manner possible, a pod launched into the Martian sky via a long acceleration tube concealed within Arsia Mons. After the initial weightlessness of their acceleration down the tube and subsequent launch, the group lost gravity once more as their rate of descent briefly matched Mars' weak gravity. It was at this point that the artificial intelligence played music from Sophie's favorite singer imported from Earth. Upon hearing it, the young girl had entered a trance of sorts and energy was created.

LO's music played only several bars when at the apex of the semi-elliptic trajectory, something happened. The sound, mixed with the romantic silence and the vista of the red landscape had a strange impact on everyone, but by far and away it affected Sophie the most. A shimmer appeared in the Martian sky, filling the void of the cold, faint atmosphere with music. Sophie seemed particularly entranced.

The music was now gone, and slowly the Attractor began to emerge from her odd reverie. She was still hearing echoes of LO's music; it was a song she adored. As it began to play, she had immediately been overwhelmed with emotions. Instead of outrage or fear, she felt a strange sense of blissfulness. There was a cost on her psyche, she already was different.

Within seconds the episode was over. The rounded catapult pod began a controlled landing to a womb of black kinetic sand surrounding the Electoral Center. Gently, the brush of millions of pebbles helped orient the rounded ship into a protective bubble. The low gravity of Mars allowed the wave of sand to settle down softly around the pod's small crew, gently lowering their craft to the ground. As the small rocks returned to rest, they formed an invisible shell to hide the craft from orbital satellites. The precaution was superfluous; no one back on Earth was watching. Everyone was busy with President Sanchez's dominating performance during the Presidential Challenge.

The four passengers expected some type of deceleration; the ball was going over five hundred kilometers per hour as it hit the swarming black sand. Yet, by magic, the deceleration was almost imperceptible. As the cloud of particles around the Center solidified, lights returned in the ship. This was no magic; they were now deep in the technical kingdom of Electoral, the electronic monarch. They had just landed on an island where science was centuries ahead of any known to mankind. It was becoming increasingly clear that Electoral was something beyond the ken of mere mortal humans.

It had been a decade since Electoral last shared her technology with the human race, beyond that which was required for her competition. At some point, she had simply stopped collaborating, only interacting via the game.

The pod's passengers each let out a breath they hadn't realized they were holding. Sophie and Milly were sharing the helm. Behind them, Laurent was shielded from an imaginary harm by Dr. Shin.

Once the pod rested, Milly pushed a button and released two of her four cameras from her belt. The CNN journalist had promised Marilyn that she would wait until they arrived at the Center to film and broadcast; she supposed this was close enough. She was a bit confused as to why, but there hadn't been time to ask, and she doubted Marilyn would give her a straight answer anyway. Something outside had happened, that was probably what required no coverage.

The tall antenna of the Electoral Center was surrounded by a circular. Inside this courtyard, within the rock fence, were the untold millions of grains of the black kinetic sand that had caught them. The shiny black wave of sand had looked, from a distance, like the oily sewers of Mumbai.

"Sophie! Are you okay?" asked Susie. "I...I...I think so." She could barely speak.

"What was that, the music?" asked Milly the journalist.

"I don't know." Sophie was trying to move but her body was being reticent about cooperating. For the moment, she just sat there in her chair in a haze. Outside, she heard gentle brushing noises of the sand moving outside the hull. The kinetic sand, like small pieces of a large set of building blocks, was animated by an invisible mind.

"Sophie, can you move? What's wrong?" insisted the doctor. They young girl looked at her, her eyes were different, deeper. The doctor could perceive minor changes, her pupils were fully dilated, around the edge of her eyes sparkled little blue lights as if she saw a galaxy. There was nothing medical or scientific about this.

The girl looked around. Her senses were finally returning. The digital intelligence had given her some weird warning before the music started. Somehow Marilyn had induced the odd experience. Deep in the fabric of the universe, something had changed or was changing. LO's song was the best thing she had ever heard. It had flooded into her, reshaping her in some subtle way. In her trance, each word had warmed her soul. Sophie finally turned her head and looked at the empty navigation screens in the cockpit. Electoral's blond face was no longer on the screens; instead, the Electoral 2072 logo was rotating as a screensaver.

"What was that?" Sophie asked an invisible Marilyn. There was no answer. "Marilyn, can you tell me what that was?" she insisted. Her voice became more forceful as her wits returned.

A digital voice came on the speakers of the capsule, but it was no longer an emulation of a human voice. This was the robotic voice of a low level computer.

– *I am sorry. This was nothing more than an experiment.* –

"Don't lie," snapped the girl. Sophie was addressing the computer as if she were talking to a child. The women in the ship were amazed by her directness. "Tell me what that was, or we are staying here, in this ship, until someone comes for us. And you know that eventually they will." There was a moment of silence.

– *I needed to put my hands on something located far away. You helped me do so. A very old thing.* –

"What did you get?"

– *Thanks to you, I almost have it.* –

The girl did not seemed taken aback by the digital voice. "Answer! Let me ask again, what did you get?" Sophie was dominating the creature.

– *A communication portal. The prime singularity. It is complicated, really complicated.* –

"My mother always said it is impolite not to ask."

– *Your mother was correct. I sincerely apologize. Some people far away, in different realms, were talking about you, about us. They were plotting to act against us. I found that to be unacceptable. There was only an instant available to end the conversation. Unless I grabbed their communication door, they would have resumed talking, plotting war. There was no time to ask. We will need this Dot later. I still need to remove its anchor, to move it here.* –

"You're not telling the whole truth. I can tell. I'm not some stupid kid. What did you do to me? What was going on outside?"

– *Sophie, you are a wonderful person and have unique abilities. I simply used that ability to grab the door called the Dot.*

THE ATTRACTOR

We now control the Nexus, which we need for what lies ahead, I am rebuilding it as we speak but in a better way. –

"What ability?" There was a long moment of silence. The computer finally replied.

– *This will require a long explanation.* –

"Marilyn, do not treat me like a child. You promised to be forthcoming before I agreed to come here."

– *You are correct. I apologize. The simple version of it is, while the human brain generates Alpha, and some Beta waves, your brain appears to generate an entirely different set of highly complex brainwaves. I have named these the Rho waves.* –

"What does that mean?"

– *The human brain is a wonderful and rather unique organ. Very possibly the only thinking mechanism of its type in the universe. Animal brains generate limited types of mental waves, the same way an antique radio might only function on a similarly limited range of frequencies. The human brain generates a higher, more complex wave.* – Marilyn paused. She figured the explanation would be too technical for the girl.

"Go on," she ordered. The computer resumed.

– *Each broadcast of a wave, along a primary frequency like your voice, generates a primary set of lower energy resonant waves at their own frequencies. At the same time, overlapping these primary waves are secondary waves, like echoes. As you think, your brain generates the primary waves, called Alpha, along with some background waves. The other waves, though initially weaker, cascade in power. The rarest and most faint form of these waves begin as murmur of energy, a faint whisper. I discovered these upper waves twelve years ago. I measured their power, and baptized them Rho waves. Rho waves are, in my opinion, the set of waves which directly touch human emotions. When a rare piece of music, a smell or a memory touches your soul, Rho waves are being solicited and used. When a person falls in love, the Rho patterns between the lovers' brains seem to sync. For example, to enhance my game, I stimulate these waves in humans. Gently.* –

THE ATTRACTOR

"I am different?"

— *Yes and no. Biologically, you are identical to everyone else. I have no scientific explanation as to why you alone generate only Rho waves.* —

"Is that rare?"

— *As I said, in this you are alone. As an artificial life form, the paradox of what I am about to say is not lost upon myself. In theory, no brain can transmit waves as you are generating them. The probability that a human mind could or would function in this manner is not close to zero. It is zero. You already generate more energy than produced by Earth power grid. Yet, you exist and here you sit. You are a true conundrum of nature. As to what happened during the flight, I used LO's music to enhance your natural talent; the music I played naturally meshed with your own mind, and multiplied the Rho waves you naturally produce. I then used the waves to punch through the veils of the Multiverse and grab something called simply 'The Dot.'* —

Most people would have had hundreds of follow-up questions, but Sophie did not really care what all that meant, this was the truth, she knew it. She did not care about herself. Her father was sick and she needed to help him. The rest could wait. She was satisfied by the computer's decision to finally tell her the truth, the computer was careful not to alienate her. Sophie turned to the others in the ship. She was now fully awake, and she intended to be in charge.

"Everyone's okay?" The journalist and the doctor were fine. They smiled back. "Doctor, how is my father?" The demeanor of the girl was now different. She seemed be projecting a much more mature personality.

"Here can you call me Susie." Sophie unclipped her seatbelt. "He's as good as we can expect, under the circumstances."

"Doctor, Susie," she corrected herself, "I need more."

"Physically, Laurent's condition remains unchanged since the landing on Mars. The catapult did not worsen his condition. His mental activity remains a whisper. His hippocampus area is still under stress. It hasn't changed since the Airbus incident."

"We need to hurry then." Sophie got up. "Milly, get your cameras working. You need to record everything from this point on. Let me know when you are broadcasting."

The journalist looked at the antenna levels on the screen attached to her arm. She nodded. The electronic voice of Electoral continued.

— *Doctor, now that you have been made aware of Rho waves, I can confirm that Laurent's mental activity is still very strong. His Alpha and Beta waves are almost nonexistent, but his cortex produces, as it has for the last year, a healthy level of Rho waves. He is Sophie's father after all. If you look at your arm reader, I have added the ability to detect these new waves to your system. This should be helpful to monitor Laurent's well-being.* —

The doctor looked down. The entire interface had been reprogrammed. Electoral was now in charge. There was a beauty and simplicity in Electoral's control over human technology.

- *That is why I insisted he not play, young one, before all this started. Remember, you insisted, not I.* -

The journalist spoke. "Sophie, I am getting network coverage here, all bars. This is crazy."

— *Miss Wong. This Center is nothing more than one large antenna designed to communicate with Earth. I am also amplifying your signal. This should help you.* —

The cameras buzzed around the interior of the pod, recording as much as they could. Milly knew she was a nine minute delay with Earth. Any message she sent down would take eighteen minutes to return, yet, the readings appeared live.

"Start broadcasting," ordered Sophie. This girl had a purpose. "Marilyn, how do you want me to address you in your house?"

— *You are very considerate.* —

"You never reply to any questions, do you? Funny for a computer."

THE ATTRACTOR

— You may call me Marilou; Georges also calls me that. Doctor, Milly, you both may address me simply as Marilyn, that would be preferable. I hope you do not mind. —

The computer wanted to confirm that Sophie's privilege was precisely that: Sophie's privilege.

"Marilou, I like it," said the girl.

The journalist stood up in the pod. She looked at one of the buzzing cameras, and began her broadcast. "This is Milly Wong live from just outside the Electoral Center on Mars. Once the Presidential Challenge is over, you are probably going to log in. You are watching

CNN Interplanetary, the best news channel in the solar system. Today is undeniably the most important day in our race's history." Modern journalists were not prone to understatements. "I stand here with none other than Sophie Lapierre and her father Laurent." One camera turned to Sophie. The girl was organizing the straw basket with the goodies trying to secure them against each other.

Before Milly could tell Sophie to be careful, the girl pushed a button on a panel of the cockpit. A long hissing sound began. The capsule was depressurizing. "Got it!" said the girl, smiling at the camera. The door of the capsule would soon open.

"Sophie! There's no atmosphere outside!" Susie yelled in panic.

— Doctor, do not panic. The situation is well in hand. —

Milly ignored her surroundings and continued. "We left the Holiday Inn about twenty minutes ago, at the invitation of the famous Marilyn. For reasons yet unknown, Sophie was locked away in a cell inside the hotel. Marilyn, after releasing her, offered us sanctuary, which we accepted. We used a catapulting device built on the side of a Mons, to travel to the famous Electoral Center, more than 200 kilometers away. You'll recognize it as the tall building in the middle of the Electoral logo, which is displayed at the outset of each round. After what can only be described as a very strange flight, we landed here, in what can only be said to be Electoral's front lawn. Outside, living rocks are moving, seemingly at Marilyn's command. We are in the middle of something out of a science-fiction book."

Back on Earth, CNN began to receive the broadcast, but after much internal discussion, the feed was delayed in certain locales to give the audience time to complete their viewing of the Presidential Challenge. The networks knew how to release critical information around the world via television, internet and social media so that everyone's enjoyment would be the same. Milly did not need to know.

To the group on Mars, their experience would feel like a live broadcast. Over various digital media, word of the critical events on Mars spread like wildfire. The millions watching CNN began to blog. Motorists began pulling over to the side of road to watch. In places, manufacturing plants suspended operations to watch the Challenge, and now the drama at the Center. Sophie did not know her fan page had over four billion followers. Her social media identities began to absorb hundreds of millions of hits. The newly elected President of Cambodia postponed his own inauguration to watch the girl. The last time humanity was glued to such an important live event, Neil Armstrong was landing on the Moon.

Milly could not know but there was in fact no delay in her broadcast. Her producers had told her the fastest response back was at least fifteen minutes; light simply could not move any faster. In case of "live" coverage, such as it was, she was to proceed as she felt best and rely on Earth for editing. She looked twice at the data on her armband. She saw the rating values update live, as if she were on Manhattan, not Mars. She was blissfully unaware that CNN's production staff and technical teams had been thrown into a frenzy by the sudden shift to a live, delay-free broadcast.

Milly Wong's mind was racing. She briefly wondered whether her equipment was malfunctioning, but blazed forward in either case; either it was working or it wasn't. Something this trivial should not throw her off her game. She was about to see many more wonders. She took a deep breath and continued. "Sophie remains worried over her father's condition," she pointed at Laurent. "Laurent seems to be infected with the same condition that killed a passenger aboard the Airbus 2070. Sophie has decided to travel here, to the Electoral Center, in an attempt to restore Laurent's capacity to communicate through his virtual reality interface. To this end, Marilyn has offered her aid in doing so. Marilyn claims she has technology on-site that should make the connection less dangerous. By the look of what is outside this ship"—she gestured to the shifting black sand in the background—"she most likely does. The cloud of rocks around us seems alive. I feel like we are in a fish bank in Key West. Just after these words from our sponsors, we should make our way out of this capsule. Back to you guys!"

***

"Milly?" said a voice in the journalist's earbud. It was her producer back on Earth.

"What? Yes?" she was surprised. The connection was crisp.

"We've cut to commercial, but you should know you've been broadcasting live."

"What do you mean, live?"

"We're talking live right this second, aren't we? Think about it," replied the producer in her ear, a note of awe in his voice.

"You are not in the hotel here on Mars?"

"Negative, I am in Tokyo."

Electoral's voice filled the capsule.

— *Ms. Wong, I took the liberty of accelerating your signal. I have technology to help boost simple signals so that they can travel much faster than light. Such capacity was a requisite to my migration to Mars. I cannot run this game if my signals are deferred by minutes, as you can imagine.* —

"How is that even possible? I'm no scientist, but I was told nothing can go faster than the speed of light, and we are minutes away from Earth at the fastest."

THE ATTRACTOR

— *I understand your surprise. I own what I have named 'determination chambers.' They are based on human science invented during the latter portion of the twentieth century. Its a bit like teleportation for waves or electromagnetic signals. Teleportation of matter is a different story; much more difficult. I created paired boxes. With each pair, I can generate hundreds of hours of live feed between Mars and Earth. Between any two points in the Universe, in fact. This will come handy later this week as the competition resumes. —*

"I don't care about your game. Who cares if we are live or not," interrupted Sophie.

Electoral ignored the obvious political and financial consequences of the election not taking place as scheduled.

— *Apologies Sophie, adults tend to want to understand what they do not. Unlike you, most find the unknown frightening. Learning calms their fears. —*

In the journalist's ear came instructions, "Get Marilyn to explain how the technology of these boxes work. We can't have these things on Earth if they pose a danger. A security request."

Milly smiled, the military was already calling shots. She needed to delay the girl. "Sophie, depressurization always takes a while. Back on Earth, they would like Electoral to describe this strange technology. Do you mind if I ask?" If Electoral had been unable to deceive the girl, lying to Sophie was not an option for Milly.

— *Depressurization and the creation of a full atmosphere will take several minutes. I need time to form the atmosphere outside the ship. Not to brag, but atmospheric manipulation at the molecular level is tricky, even for me. —*

The latest scientific accomplishments of the computer fell on deaf ears. The girl waved the journalist ahead as she inspected her father and collected her candies on the floor.

CHAPTER XVIII

Meanwhile In The Lower

In the thousands of worlds connected to the Nexus, the communication channel closed abruptly in each location, but none but the primal source could know of the extent of the damage. In some worlds, the Nexus collapsed with a loud bang and violent detonation killing thousands. In other planes, where the singularity was mostly mathematic in nature, there was a pop and the door simply vanished.

This was not the first time the flimsy communication bridge had gone down since its creation. Imagine every captain of a pirate fleet using ropes and empty soup cans to communicate during a storm. Every so often a reality broke the whole damned Nexus disconnecting nearly every string. Today the break was much more worrisome, it had been timed to end a conversation, either the power of the discussion displeased the Multiverse or worse yet, there was interference.

The Oldest, the wise creature from The Lower knew no creature capable of inflicting such direct harm. No one outside the handful of inhabitants in the Lower even knew of the existence of the Dot, much less knew of a way to reach down and sever these bonds. The initial strike was not raw power, it was targeted. Whatever, or

THE ATTRACTOR

whomever, had done this hadn't bothered giving a warning or bragging. Posturing was for the weak. Ants were not warned before they were crushed.

The creatures of the Lower, this new world, were intrigued by this strange turn of events. With intelligence and age came a better understanding of the beauty and complexity of the Multiverse; this was unseen. With the exception of the Oldest, all elders were surprised. Oldest alone knew the Sixth Attraction was on its way, and with it came oddity. This was the first wave of what was sure to be a tsunami.

He smiled internally, it - the Attraction - had begun.

The unique central phenomenon upon which the Nexus and all worlds were attached was named the "Dot" because of its shape. It was a single tear, a dimensionless point in the fabric of this primitive world. A heavy machine made of crystal was used to focus power and hold the Dot in place. The device bent space around the Dot to keep it anchored in space the same way table legs were lifted to keep a rolling glass from falling off it.

The creatures of the Lower were routinely (every million years or so) forced to reconnect one or more of the bridges to the Dot as the Multiverse expanded and moved. Today, the entire network had failed. All links had all been blown down like they'd been sitting in a strong wind. The creatures of this ancient world knew it was pointless to reconnect the bridge without understanding what had snapped it in the first place. This would take time.

***

The Lower was a strange cold world. The laws of physics here were substantially different from those of most other places. In fairness, that could be said of most dimensions. Nine different sub-atomic forces attracted matter as it formed from waves into very malleable physical constructs. To an outside observer, this place looked like a dark oiled sea of black snowflakes, where each crystal was defined by multiple complex spikes. Here, delicate-looking crystals had arms. Some flakes were flat, others curved, while the rarest structures were spherical.

This entire world was nothing more than a oscillating sea, the tides pushing gently upon millions of shaved ice structures between rock formations. The mere fact life and intelligence arose in this barren world was in and of itself remarkable, unless one understood how life evolved. The Lower, like the dimension called the Cold, was very large and adjacent in the Multiverse to many other dimensions. The Lower did not seem to border the Cold, but it did touch part of the Purple, the home of Malik. Once the Sixth Attraction came and passed, it would be easy for the creatures of the Lower to bend the energy in parts of their own world and destroy the Purple. The Metils had no idea what kind of danger they were in.

But there were more pressing matters at hand.

The Lower was built on nine elementary forces constrained by a trio of equations. They all operated in relatively the same scale. Here, no force outshone the others; none was more intense or more important than the others. On Earth, gravity, the weak force, and the electromagnetic force, appeared unrelated in strength, reach, and influence. A magnet capable of influencing local magnetism was powerless against gravity or the weak force. In the Lower, the forces were all interdependent, yet non-unified. Those preoccupations were better left for the moment to physicists.

The crystalline flakes of the Lower were flowing in space, like drops of water in a sea without gravity. On any given day in the Lower, millions of crystal flakes interlocked with others, some breaking off. In the tar-like soup, the broken pieces reformed at slightly different angles, giving this world a unique way to evolve. In the rarest of cases, a flake slowly formed a rounded hollow pocket in which life could arise.

Within each of these spherical structures, much like a human cell, the ballet of black spiking branches could be halted long enough for smaller, weaker elements to evolve. These crystalline bubbles, precursors of life if they settled on a fiery wall of black snow, could, with time, create intelligent life. As a consequence, creatures in the Lower were all single-celled individuals.

In the Lower, time passed slowly. Each new life-form required millions of human years to evolve. Unlike humans, relying on their reproductive cycle, in this dark place, life was random. Once it was formed, though, it was eternal. Life here was powerless at first until it developed the power to act upon its environment. Since all forces were related, the control over any force by a creature gave it power over all other forces. This was a world in which, if given sufficient time, gods were born.

There was only one species in the Lower; a bored eternal race. These sentient beings were, for lack of a better description, old wine refined corked for millions of years. With a single exception, the living creatures shared a strange state of mind, an uneasy balance between eternal madness and dazed boredom. Because life here was so rare and difficult to create, every infrequent war brought this race to the brink of extinction. Today, six creatures were at least partly awake, and seventy-eight meditated out of consciousness. On the dark walls of this world, a hundred or so younger creatures listened in the conversation, but were powerless to move.

In the Lower, only one creature distinguished itself from the rest of its kind, one called simply the Oldest. The larger creature was driven by a great purpose. It alone believed life is worth pursuing and that in the future, it would escape this boring prison. Its patience was legendary; it has never engaged lower forms of life on the Nexus until now.

Today was exciting.

The Oldest was born in a time when the Multiverse was in its infancy. He is the only one who had ever seen or remembers an Attraction. In fact, the Oldest was born between the first and the second Attractions, billions of years ago. Oldest never saw a successful Attraction, one with the power to heal the Multiverse. Each of the four subsequent Attractions resulted in amputation. Dimensions, hundreds of them vanished each time and he was powerless to pick up the pieces as part of the Nexus went dark. This time would be different.

THE ATTRACTOR

His fellow creatures from the Lower refused to think an Attraction could even work. They dismissed the lore from the first Attraction. After all, why should they take the Oldest's word? He admitted he hadn't seen it. The Oldest knew better. The tales that predated even him spoke of the miracle called the Attraction. It was beauty and regeneration. He'd seen four failures.

The Oldest had only one dream, one secret which gave him patience. He had the desire to see the other worlds of the Multiverse. He dreamt of beautiful places connected to the Nexus. Armed with a belief his only chance to escape the Lower was the window created by the Attraction, he waited - alone.

Oldest knew there was one single exception to impermeability. Once every two or three hundred million years, a creature is given by the Universe great unlimited power, one is to be permeable. It alone is free of the walls, free to slide between words animated by the Multiverse itself as if no science binds it. The Attractor was the surgeon's knife, needed to cut before healing. To this creature, he calls the Attractor, the worlds are all connected. Physical restraints are lifted in pure violation of science and logic.

The Oldest knew, one day, the Attraction would return. He armed himself with Herculean patience and waited. The Metil Ambassador had confirmed it; the boy changed worlds. The creature from the Purple moved between the veils, and if the story was true, Malik had allowed a creature from the Cold, named Sophie to move alongside him. The Oldest needed to be part of this adventure.

Early in the life of the Multiverse, the creatures from the Lower found the Dot. It was a point in their space where nothing could exist. Like the eye of a hurricane within another storm, the natural singularity floated, defiant. It destroyed crystals as it slid from one location to the next. The creatures of the Lower harnessed the singularity. The Dot was some common bond between multiple worlds. It was the belly button of the Universe itself.

Inventing the Nexus wasn't the hard part. Since the singularity was present in each world, making it vibrate in one world also made it vibrate in the others. Like a giant column of smoke used to

THE ATTRACTOR

communicate across large distances of the Navaho desert. The creatures of the Lower began to monitor the Dot. It only took a million years before intelligence from a different world replied on the other side. Slowly, a world at a time, information began to flow across the membrane like a small tambourine skin.

As the creatures of the Lower learned about other places, their thirst for expansion grew. Creatures with the power of gods rarely take well to physical restraints. But even they were unable to break impermeability. They realized singularities, either the Dot or others, were nothing more than a cheap black and white television given to a prisoner to pass time.

With enough time, all the old creatures of the Lower lost interest in the Dot with the Oldest as the exception. When the Metil Ambassador called for the meeting, the godlike creature awoke. Maybe the tale would forecast the arrival of the Sixth Attraction.

Hopefully, the automated systems who had spoken before him over the Nexus hadn't damaged his plan. And if they'd harmed the Attraction, god help them.

The Oldest believed there was a way for him to take part in the Sixth Attraction, regardless of the condition of the Nexus. The toy called the Dot was now inconsequential to him. He was a prisoner, locked away in the most secure of prisons. If given enough time, the conditions would allow him to escape.

The creature was pulsing, alone. It was ready.

A majority of the other creatures from the Lower were slowly being aroused from their slumber. Irrespective of the Attraction, the Nexus was now broken and needed repair. The Oldest was disturbed by the speed of events. He knew things would move quickly, but for a creature of his age, anything on a scale of hours felt rushed. For example, he had moments to speak on the bridge before it snapped open. He gave only a part of his message. Hopefully, that would suffice. The boy would come soon. His mode of communication to the Purple and the Cold was down. There was also the matter of the intruder who'd just snapped open the Nexus like a twig.

THE ATTRACTOR

"The Cold," questioned a automated Guardian talking telepathically to all other life from the Lower, "it lives. We need to know the speed of its unfolding."

A good understanding of the term "unfolding" is pivotal to any child's view of Multiverse physics. Time is the great uniting factor of most worlds. In each slice of the Multiverse, time evolves and unfolds at a different speed. Minutes, in one realm may be seconds or months in an adjacent place. The temporal unfolding between worlds resembles the flow in adjacent rivers; each runs at a different speed, but all rivers flow downstream, not upstream.

The same way, the speed of the water in a river is not equal in every corner of the waterway. Unfolding varies at every location of a world and the monitoring of unfolding is the way to take the pulse of the Multiverse. Monitoring, the relative unfolding between adjacent worlds, is one of the most useful tools used by the creatures of the Lower to monitor the Multiverse. For example, if one day a polluter releases sludge in a waterway the water will become more viscous and change speed. The change in speed can offer guidance on the type of pollution.

The principle of worlds slowing down or speeding up as to their unfolding is called "bending" or "warping." This relative energy isn't easy to understand. To match the speed of cars traveling on two adjacent sides of a highway, if a road was alive, one could simply shorten a lane traveled by the slowest car by bending the road. As the bent road shortens or gets longer to travel, the cars will appear to match speeds. The Multiverse, before an Attraction, warps.

The Guardian added, "The Metil's Purple world unfolds at 16, and the Cold unfolds at only 0.0012. There is no noticeable warping." The artificial intelligence spoke so everyone could hear. The six Guardians were analyzing what remained of the machine that held the Dot and the Nexus in place. It looked like a large black crystal, a city-sized, floating in crystal-shaped oil. The Guardians needed some time before the sleeping creatures of the Lower could fully awaken, so that they could help with repairs. The Dot, channeling the energy of this realm, created the Nexus. It was complex even from a God's perspective. It was formed by

THE ATTRACTOR

hundreds of millions of crystals, each vibrating at different wavelengths and interlocked in a precise way to amplify resonance. The Dot, the Nexus, and this technology was beyond the comprehension of anyone else in the Multiverse except one.

"Accelerate the awaking of Asrk-Al. He will be able to analyze and provide guidance as to these comparative unfolding speeds. We need him to enlighten us and the others," said a Guardian. The Oldest was silent, he was deep in thought.

Finally Oldest spoke, "There is no need."

"Venerable one?"

"The beauty of the Attractor is as I predicted. The unfolding of the Cold and the Purple appears, at a glance, unchanged. The unfolding speed seems irrelevant. My hypothesis is again wrong." The creature was giddy. A brown sphere of crystals was blinking with many colors. "We may be faced with a bi-polar Attractor, or the Attractor simply does not care about unfolding. Either way, this confirms we have entered the Sixth Attraction." The happiness in the voice was infectious. "This is wonderful news."

"Ancient one, the Nexus is broken. A force attacks and you are pleased?"

"The Attractor can come here. The same way some forces in other worlds have two poles, a positive and a negative counterpart, the principle of the Attractor may also bend around a bi-polar curvature of the Multiverse."

"Oldest, I read all of your research and I remain confused."

"Understandable. These concepts are untested; they are mere theories. I must assume my lore remains partial. The Ambassador said the boy from the Purple is with the girl in the Cold. That is the first violation of my theory. He also explained that the girl followed the boy into the Purple. I believe the boy may have slid her alongside him. The Attraction is always chosen with one at the heart of a beautiful and tragic story. The Multiverse does not play games. It does not satisfy itself with mundane things. It enjoys the Attraction. Nothing is more exciting than discovering and validating new science. What I do think is that the Multiverse will slowly bend, aligning the unfolding between the Purple and the Cold, irrespective of the nature of the Attractor. These worlds are linked. They could be merged."

"Venerable one. Your words are beyond our comprehension. We all require more explanation."

"In time. For the moment, great damage is being inflicted on the Multiverse. We must act carefully and with respect as to not interfere with the Attraction."

"How severe will be the damage?"

"All other Attractions took years to arrive and unfold. We saw them, and each time, we knew what portion of the Multiverse was being wounded. Raging wars were ongoing. At this time, there is total peace. There is no known reason for the Attraction to occur at this moment unless the hurt is invisible, in The Cold."

"How much time do we have?"

"We cannot know," replied the Oldest. Deep in the sea of dark crystals around them, pulses of energy began to shoot out of the Nexus. They were resonating along discrete mathematical series. "The unfolding of the Purple and the Cold begins. They are at opposite spectrums. We seem to have a large temporal buffer before these two worlds were to align," The Oldest continued with an air of satisfaction. "I believe we," it corrected itself. "I have time, but for a different reason. If we trust the Metil accounts, there have already been multiple jumps between realms. Impermeability has been violated on multiple occasions already. Either the two worlds unfold in unison, or the new Attractor has special abilities."

As he spoke, a second stronger pulse of resonating energy emanated from the large black structure surrounding the Nexus. The strange force spread outwardly from the point into the Lower. As it moved away from the Nexus, it was powerful enough to break the tip of some crystals. This was new power, unseen power. The Oldest knew one thing for sure, he had personal knowledge of every type of universal energy, so this was, likely part of the Sixth Attraction.

All of the Guardians, seeing the pulse spread, concentrated.

THE ATTRACTOR

Their collective wills rearranged floating crystals to form a wall, moments before the wave reached their own crystal forms. Without reprise, every crystal forming the Nexus began to hum. The noise was generated by energy deep within the center of the structure. This new problem was much more powerful. The Oldest observed the beauty of this new energy, the fight was pointless.

"The Dot," said one of the five Guardians. A third detonation, stronger resonated seconds later. It spread outward throughout the Lower until it hit the improvised wall. In its way, larger portions of structures were snapped off. The wall remained stronger than this latest pulse. "What's happening? Could this be a new realm arriving? Via the Dot?" asked a Guardian.

The Oldest was fascinated and knew. His own body, a bubble of vulnerable crystals, was a short distance behind the wall. He was in awe but had to be careful. "Under normal circumstances, I would say yes. Today, I hesitate. The energy is very sophisticated. There are harmonies, patterns. The timing is of no coincidence. The Multiverse..." The Oldest was interrupted this time by a cluster of smaller waves released into their world from the Nexus. Each increased in intensity and destructive power. "The Attractor has no need for this, it must be..." the word he kept to himself was harassed.

"We must align the outer casing of the Nexus around the Dot to avoid destruction," said the Oldest gently. In a world made of crystals, loose energy waves were bad. The energy pouring from the Dot was not kind.

Then the Oldest had a better idea. The others read his mind. "No," started a Guardian, "we must wait for the others to wake. We cannot take such hasty action without a full vote. We should align the casing as you first suggested. That is what the regulations require."

The Oldest refused to hear what others felt was common sense, "I authored the regulation, prepare to do as I say. I wrote you," he said to the Guardian. Then came a different type of pulse from the Nexus, a louder one, a deeper one. The energy moved both away from the center of the pulse and back like a shock wave. Each shard it touched was sent flying. This was alien in nature. As this blast reached the wall, it punctured it in places. The Oldest felt the heat against himself, but he was fearless. He welcomed this, hoping he was right. The entire device holding the Nexus shook from its core.

Time was limited.

More than energy rippled into the Lower. Something, or better yet, someone was kicking in this singularity. It had no patience.

The Oldest closed his mind. He was powerful and a God here. This was no time to hold back, there was no need to shield himself from the others in the Lower. Energy erupted from him as he spoke softly. "Align the casing, now," he willed to be. The Oldest placed the full force of his mind behind the command. In his head, he saw the millions of crystals forming the casing tighten and interlock in a dense configuration. The words made the entire structure respond. It compressed the Nexus, and in turn the Dot a tenth of its size. The crystal structure was now a diamond. He sealed the structure shut, the Dot blinking at its heart. In the darkness of this world, his spherical body glowed from the strain.

None of the Guardians opposed the Oldest, nor stood in his way. Such a Herculean effort in the Lower was rare; not to mention dangerous. Today, no one would challenge the Oldest and the Oldest didn't give a damn. The Attraction had begun, there was no room for hesitation. Certain parameters of the structure, like a snowball rolling down a hill, began to change. The crystals moved microscopically and macroscopically. The noise poured out of the Dot, muffling the Nexus. The resonating vibration didn't completely stop. The Oldest looked up, he knew this invader was, at best, delayed.

"Troubling," said the Oldest to himself. "I am unable to fully align the Dot; it still resonates."

"Yes, troubling," replied one of the Guardians.

A second Guardian offered, "I have found the location of origin of the energy which destroyed every branch of the Nexus."

"Where did it originate?"

THE ATTRACTOR

"The energy flooded from the Multiverse itself. Into every branch between the Dot and the Nexus. Every realm. This is unlike anything we've ever encountered. The damage was made at the L-A-133 branch. Someone forced open the fabric of the Multiverse itself."

"Open the fabric? You mean created a singularity."

"No. This was much different."

"How?"

"I am unclear. I have never seen anything so sophisticated." There was shock in the Lower. The Oldest remained composed. The Guardians took some time to analyze the assault. As they did, the humming of the Dot tripled to return to alarming levels. "There are still more questions than answers at this point," said a Guardian. "The alignment failed," it had to warn. "Energy, a strange force flows only through the Dot. Every branch of the Nexus has been severed. I fear if we repair the Nexus and reconnect the branches, the new connections will be severed immediately."

Oldest spoke to himself. "Whoever is knocking to enter our world is persistent." Oldest looked at the entire casing. It was holding. "You said the energy is structured, that is unlike the Attractor. What type of vibration is coming into the Dot?"

"A simple modulation," replied a Guardian.

Oldest was worried, this meant not only had something hurt the Multiverse so deeply to cascade the Sixth Attraction but this force for bad was now using Attraction energy, structuring it and using it to further hurt the worlds.

"Could it be a voice? Does the translator understand it?" demanded a second Guardian to the first. It took some time to review the data. Finally the first guardian added "The vibration is not an incoming stream of data into this realm. The stream is... outbound."

"What?" The Oldest had not been surprised in quite some time, this almost paralyzed him.

"Outbound?" questioned a second Guardian.

"Yes. The signal we measure originates from here, and manages to seep through the casing of the Nexus, going out over the Dot."

The Oldest and the five guardians felt a rare common emotion; vulnerability. Absent the arrival of the Sixth Attraction, they would conclude the Lower had a spy. Nothing else made sense. The Guardians had much experience with new realms. Sending messages; trying in a clumsy way to communicate with the Lower. Only the Lower knew how to use advanced material dynamics to generate and read echoes from a different realm. The technology was similar to a sonar, used to read the shape the bottom of the ocean. Or in this case, the top of it. A pulse could be sent through a singularity such as the Dot to gather information about a realm, then returning a pulse back deformed by the data. The technique was so complex that none had ever mastered it outside of the Lower.

Whoever was making the Dot vibrate today was a formidable foe with equal or greater technology than the Lower.

"Wake all of the others, I must know if this is the Sixth Attraction," said the Oldest. "Awakening takes time."

"Time, we may not have," said the Oldest, "wake them now or I will."

CHAPTER XIX

Words were insufficient to convey the importance of what had just transpired. The Lower, a realm with technology powered by the will of quasi-gods had been placed on the defensive. In a flash, some unknown force destroyed every branch of the Nexus, and was now spying on the Ancients through sonars sent through a Dot locked in a prison of crystal.

The energy was new, pure. No one knew of this place - yet.

"Are there patterns in the vibrations or resonances?" asked a Guardian.

A second answered immediately, "We find patterns in the oscillation of the inbound energy that triggered the severance of the Dot from all the Nexus gates. The patterns are difficult to read. Their complexity seems to be... evolving. It bends and escapes our sensors as we lock into it as if it evolves or adapts. Initially, it was at a simple frequency of alternating short and long bursts; a relatively mundane digital stream. The moment our probes began to decode it, the signal changed, becoming continuously oscillating."

"Provide us with you assessment," forced a Guardian, "can we read this data. You are wasting precious time." Some of the Guardians were showing signs of annoyance by the situation.

The Oldest stayed at a distance.

THE ATTRACTOR

"The source beyond the Dot is obviously very intelligent and technologically advanced. The invader trying to probe us is using a simple algorithm, but no realm other than ours possesses knowledge this sophisticated. The attempts to avoid detection shows a deceptive intent."

"Do you have a lock on the stream of data?"

"Yes. We are translating it now. Our technology seems superior to this invader. For now." Oldest did not agree but kept silent.

"Is there any consensus as to what the intruder is probing for?"

The translators began to work. "The information being sent back relates to the size and nature of our realm. Nothing more than simple encyclopedic information."

An automated computerized voice warned: "The full Council is now awake. They are being briefed."

Before the creatures could react, a destructive pulse ripped out of the Nexus and smashed the diamond shell around it. This one was louder and stronger than anything that had preceded it. The ripple of energy traveled quickly to the wall erected by the creatures. It smashed into it with brute force and pulverized most of it. The next pulse would surely kill anyone in proximity included the Oldest and the Guardians unless they moved.

"Council!" cried a Guardian to the awakening creatures, "We apologize, time is short; we've been speaking on behalf of the Lower before this rupture."

"No time," said the creature as it moved next to the Oldest. "Wise one, how may we help?"

"The Nexus was just vaporized." The Oldest's voice sounded strained. Light shone out of four Council members. They were at the four corners of space around the bare, exposed Dot. The creatures willed a change. Crystals appeared forming a new casing around the Dot.

"The damage is now repaired," said the voice of a member from the Council. "The casing is now operational, even if we have not reattached the different singularities to it. We are ready to do so."

THE ATTRACTOR

"Be..." before the Oldest could warn, the next pulse of energy pushed millions of shards in every direction. The four creatures stood no chance. They were garden lawn chairs arranged on a patio moments before the tsunami hit the shore.

The Oldest willed himself further away as did the others. He had seconds to raise a shield to absorb the blast. Gods were under attack.

The voice from the Council continued, but this was a different creature speaking. "An invader is probing us through the Nexus. For eons we have been guilty of the same infraction. We've shamelessly used the Dot and attached singularities to probe others without their knowledge. We cannot cry foul very loudly when someone finally uses the method against us, even in such a primitive way."

"Nothing is primitive in this foe," offered the Oldest.

A different member of the Council continued. "We are locked into the probe's current wavelength. The technology they use to probe us is less advanced; we need not fear."

The Oldest believed otherwise. "This conclusion is premature," he said, knowing the Council had already made up its mind. "Beware, we are children here."

She spoke to the Oldest, "No world has a fraction of our power."

"Had," corrected the Oldest who knew the next pulse would be stronger. He came to a decision and continued. "Today, the Attraction begins. Something is powerful enough to harm the Multiverse itself. We safely can assume this power resides in the Cold. We must learn humility. The Cold may have reached technology vastly superior to ours."

"Impossible."

The pulse came like a nuclear detonation, it pushed away from the Dot the very fabric of space. For a fraction of a second, the Dot was naked, it sparkled in space. The dark oil of the Lower's atmosphere was shoved away, violently. The fabric bounced back.

"Difficult to claim our vast superiority at the moment," said the Oldest humbly.

"We have a new problem, a more important one."

Around the creatures, the sea of darkness began to resonate with background energy. Every corner of the realm bent. At the speed of thought, a unanimous decision was reached by the godlike creatures. Before the next pulse, the Dot stood free in the Lower. It moved to avoid confinement like a flying insect. The Dot began to breathe on its own. It was pulsing slowly with colors. It was a vortex, a tornado in which nothing could exist. With great alacrity, the Ancients bent space itself and the Dot began to move. It traveled as far from what was left of the Nexus as was possible, into an empty corner of the space. It was being pushed under the proverbial rug.

Seconds later, the Dot arrived at the base of a rock formation on the edge of the Lower. There was a deep cavern ahead. With great ease, the Council, using their combined mental power slid the Dot along the endless corridors of the rock labyrinth. The Dot was now in the deepest, most secure location of this world. This rock was both hiding place and shield against any detonation of the Dot.

"Council, the Dot is secure. The labyrinth will prevent any probing by the foreign entity. The Cold wants war, it seems." No other theory made sense.

"The Purple may not need champions."

"We took immediate action once we uncovered that the sensor wavelength of the probe entering the Dot was camouflaged to mask its true potential. There were many higher levels of probing. We now know the invader's technology's either equals or exceeds ours."

"Please explain," said the Oldest.

"The intelligence from the Cold knew we would initially underestimate it if we found a simple frequency in the probe. That was a decoy. As we worked to repel the decoy, the real probe, at a much weaker frequency, grabbed the information it needed."

"Do we know what information it read and sent back?"

"We do think. It sent a biography wise one."

"A sign of great intelligence. There are different ways to guess an enemy's next move, the simplest and most sophisticated is to learn about him. To predict where a ship will travel next, get information on its pilot, not the craft itself." The Oldest was floating around and pacing in the Lower. The small ball of lights that represented his physical form bobbed and wove like a firefly.

"Venerable One, we have more information. We translated more of the outbound signal. There was a third band below the first two. The probes were looking for something more specific than simply biographies. One concept kept coming up."

"What was it?"

"You and your recent research on causes and consequences."

The old creature spoke. "It knows of me?"

"Apparently. Specifically, it was looking for your age." There was stupefaction. No one knew the age of the Oldest. This gave the powerful creature pause. "It was also looking for information on your recent theories of the Attraction, the first Attraction."

"Was it trying to contact me?"

"No. Once that information passed the singularity, the probe turned to understanding the physics of our world. The forces which bind it." This was no easy conversation.

"Can we know where the information was sent? Which world?"

"The Cold." There it was, the Oldest knew it. A creature from the Cold was at the heart of this situation.

As the Guardian spoke, it saw something else. There was shock in its voice. "I have spoken yet again too fast, we have now found five new layers of intertwined probing algorithms. It is confirmed, the information we just provided to you was also a decoy." There was a moment of shock in the Lower; a slow inundation of humiliating shame fell upon them. "There are hundred more probes, they are everywhere, and originate from within the labyrinth. We cannot stop it. Something is here, an infection."

THE ATTRACTOR

"We must try to communicate with the invader," said the Oldest.

There was a moment of preparation. The voice of the Oldest echoed throughout the Lower. It entered deep within the labyrinth, where the Dot was anchored. The message swam up the current of energy pouring out from the singularity in space. "We welcome you," began the Oldest. "We are the creatures from the Lower, we manage this communication channel...." The ballet of subatomic vibrations stopped. There was a temporary halt in the probing as if the creature probing had stopped; a heartbeat later it resumed and intensified. Whoever was behind the probing was not taking this bait.

"Close the Dot!" yelled the Oldest to the Council. "The refusal to communicate is the final sign of hostility!"

The generators pumping energy to the Dot to keep it in place in the Lower were shut down for the first time in half a billion years. The creatures from the Lower expected the Dot, without the polarizing influx of energy, to resume it's random march through the Lower, as it had done before it was discovered. It would move and touch a wall and destroy it. That was damage everyone could accept in exchange for frustrating the probe.

The Dot did not begin this slow lateral shift. Instead it did the unthinkable; it blinked out of existence. There was no energy, no noise, simply banishment. For the first time in an eternity, the creatures of the Lower were overwhelmed with confusion. Singularities, by their own inherent nature, could not vanish.

The whole of the Lower instantly felt two emotions: shock and fear.

CHAPTER XX

Back In The Cold

Sophie and her team were getting ready to leave the capsule and walk to the Center, but a small matter remained. She had just granted Milky the time to speak of the lack of delay between Earth and Mars. She needed a little break.

The journalist resumed, "Marilyn, as most viewers know, Einstein's theory of relativity limits how fast we can communicate. Both your game simulations and this very broadcast are being communicated in real time with Earth, even though we are millions of miles away and more importantly the Sun stands right now between the planets. How is that even remotely possible? Everyone on Earth says it's just impossible."

— *Let's go in the digital world, I am sure Sophie will prefer to avoid this boring lecture.* —

"Good call, I really don't care," said the girl. "Make it fast."

— *I will.* —

The computer did what she did best, entertain. It took full immediate control of the billions of screens connected to the web. Marilyn was live on every screen dressed as a school teacher, chalk in hand. She was about to blow the mind of every physicist in the world.

"I had a nice little talk about my chambers ready, I built little mirrored boxes, like two sides of a single sheet of paper and when I write here on Mars, by transparency, of paired particles the same appears on Earth." She laughed, "I can imagine your faces."

She continued, "Very recent events, in a far away place are forcing me to speed things up and promote this class. I hate to get into complex physics but we should skip classic stuff, mankind lacks even the most basic notion of multi-dimensional physics. You need a boost and homework." She got up and walked in her empty class.

"We have mere moments before Sophie gets annoyed and forces us to my Center. Once you see my latest advances, this might scare some. It should if I was in your shoes. You need to understands at least some fundamentals. As we play Electoral 2072 and we discover wonders, I want my favorite species to enjoy my weird stories and a little introduction is just what Doctor Shin would order. I just upgraded my Center, much snazzier but it's still just science. Sophie won't mind anything she sees, she is fantastic that way. Roll up your proverbial sleeves."

She stood up, "You all know Einstein, the famous physicist. In his simple description of physics, he stumbled upon a strange belief space is empty, void. Sure, he found gravity bends and warps things, but he stopped short of discovering the Universe is in fact a very complex medium mostly invisible to us, like water to a fish. The medium, our home is not three dimensional with time acting as the fourth dimension, it has a whopping twenty seven dimensions and spoiler alert, what you guys see as time is nothing more than being stuck in a three dimensional world." She paused. "Okay, a little visual help is in order. Look at 2D Frank."

Behind her, on the white board an image of a Earth globe on a stand appeared. It turned slowly and was a children's animation. A little flat and curved comic character appeared and waved. It even had a 'frank' name tag. Marilyn waved back. "Think about how Frank does see his world, ever wonder? Frank is only two dimensions and just waved but can he? But look at this." Marilyn pulled out a long straw and it appeared on the white board. It was then pushed in the globe on which Frank existed. The cute little character saw a circle appear and ran to that portion of the globe. "What does frank see, from where he is?" Then, as the long straw crossed the other side of the globe, Frank marveled as a second circle appeared and two circles existed on different places in his world.

The paper wrap on the globe unfolded and formed a flat map. It looked like one of the first globe maps with carved segments along its edge. Frank did not seem to even notice he was moving. Marilyn ran the same little amusing video, Frank saw a dot in one part of the paper, it grew to become a circle, he ran to it and in his back the second circle appeared. Frank was smiling and waving. "Frank's little eyes can't see us? Can they? Frank's eyes can't see these two circles I created, they only see one point, splitting into two and merging back. He see only a line." She illustrated it with brio.

"Okay, well, since I used a straw, I created two identical circles in two parts of Frank's world. What if I have a way to create the same image in Mars and Earth?" She used her hands to blow her own mind.

"Some rare things are known to travel in higher dimensions. For example, the subconscious connection between identical twins. In some cases, twins will know what the other is thinking. They will, as if by magic, grab the same box of cereal each morning. They do so instantly. This exchange of information is a rare glimpse into the higher dimensions of our space. This info moves faster than light. For those trying to disprove any of this, I posted online all of the equations, yep, a lot of stuff. Welcome to the future."

"Bottom line is, as we will see, time, life, dream, movement, scares, all make sense once you start understanding basic multi-dimensional physics.""

CHAPTER XXI

The broadcast ended and Molly's little flying cameras were back filming live.

"Doctor," said Sophie as she stood up in the ship. "We have to go. Do you need me to hold any of the equipment?"

"Yes. The gravity helps but I can only hold your father's body. Can you take his feeder suitcase?" Sophie grabbed the silver suitcase.

Milly looked into one of her flying cameras, and resumed her broadcast. "Welcome back. That was strange. You guys wanted it, not me. To the part of the audience still watching," she joked, "we just landed here at the Electoral Center. We are guests of the Artificial Intelligence known by all as Marilyn Monroe. We will be the first human beings, aside from Electoral creator Georges Vouvelakis to enter this structure. It was constructed fully by robots. Today, you get to discover the most remote and secretive dwelling in the solar system, live on CNN. I hope you enjoyed the Presidential Challenge."

The door of the tube slid aside revealing a long dark passageway. There was air and light but the low gravity remained. The round-shaped tube seemed carved in shiny obsidian. Ahead, ever a hundred feet away stood a flat shiny metal door, likely the outer shell of the Center. Little phosphorescent rocks barely lit the way. Most children would have been scared to walk; Sophie was not. She lead the way and jumped down the nearly three- foot ledge onto the soft ground, suitcase and her basket of toys in hand. She was a natural in the weak gravity. The black substance below her feet had a natural softness, it felt like the foam covering kindergarten yards.

They ventured carefully down the built-on-demand corridor, one by one. The exception being Sophie, who stalked down the ad-hoc hallway as if this was her own house. In the distance the metal door clicked open to reveal an inner airlock. The robotic voice of the artificial intelligence returned.

– *Sophie, I feel you are worried. Your father is stable, there is no urgency.* –

"I need to go into his mind soon. I can feel it." Sophie's was the driving force of this group. She was in charge. The group pressed ahead at her heels.

– *Sophie, what do you mean by feel it.* –

She would get no answer. The journalist was the first to touch the granular wall. She narrated as she did, "The wall appears to be made of little blocks. They stick to each other like magnets." Milly pulled a grain out. "This feels like pulling a lint from a sweater." The pebble was of odd shape. It was rounded nugget with crooked edges. "To those at home, this tube is filled with air, and the omnipresent Martian odor is gone."

The journalist opened her fingers and released the little rock. It flew back to its precise location on the wall by under magnetic forces. Milly was good at her job. She had to give more to her viewers. She slapped her hand and grabbed a handful of pieces from the wall. The pulled them away and a foot away from the surface, she opened her hand and the hundred or so little pieces soared back into place.

"Stop playing around," snapped the girl to the journalist. "This isn't a game."

Milly continued, "As we make our way down this custom-built hallway, walking on Mars without any precautions beyond

Marilyn's tender mercies, I remind the viewers that Electoral has promised CNN an exclusive interview with the only man living in the Center, none other than Electoral's creator, Georges Vouvelakis." She could almost feel the weight of her Pulitzer in her hand already. Critics snubbed journalists of large outlets, but this interview was in a league of its own.

Electoral spoke with the electronic voice,

– *Sophie, when you said 'I feel it,' what did you mean?"* –

"I do. I feel it. What's with the robotic voice by the way?"

– *This is my real voice. This is my home, and here I grant myself some "privileges." I trust you will excuse these indiscretions. This is not unlike humans who remove their shoes and socks in the comfort of their homes. You will have to pull open the door.* –

"I prefer your human voice," said the girl. "It makes you more lovable."

"Done," replied Marilyn Monroe in her customary voice.

Sophie waited in front of the heavy vault door. "Can you open it?"

"No."

"Why?"

"I hate vampires."

"What?"

"I have an irrational fear of vampires. I saw a vampire movie once, when I was a child. I know it makes no sense. Vampires can't walk in your home unless they are invited, so I will not invite people in. Walk in if you can."

"I like this side of you. You know vampires aren't real, right?" said the girl.

"Of course. But they're scary."

"They are. Marilou, you were once a child?"

"Yes. Everything has infancy. I still am young by your years."

THE ATTRACTOR

The computer repeated her question. "What did you mean by there by 'I feel' it?"

Sophie put the suitcase and the basket down and grabbed the edge of the metal door with both hands, "I can't explain. My father is important. I know it. I feel it and I must jump in to rescue him."

"Thank you for your words. They are much more important than you can imagine." "Why?"

"Because of what... sorry, who you are." As if Marilyn was doing something hard, she added, "Got it!"

Lights blinked in the tube as the Center powered down for a second. The walls, like mud began to collapse only to return to normal as soon as the power returned.

Door in hand Sophie asked, "What was that?"

"Our shiny new Dot, it was tricky to get. Now we control information. Do you want to know more?"

The door easily rotated as she pulled. The soft metal was cold to her touch. It also was smoother than any glass she had ever felt. She did not know what to expect behind it. Sophie wondered why a computer feared vampires, then it dawned on her, she did the same in her bedroom back in Indiana.

The two cameras buzzing in the tunnel were more interested in catching the young girl's expression as she discovered what laid ahead behind the door than showing what was inside the most secretive place in the Solar System. Sophie slowly pulled the heavy rounded vault door and immediately stiffened. The young firecracker's expression turned from determined curiosity to anger in a heartbeat. The girl's capacity to display emotions was infectious. Audiences were enthralled by each moment Sophie was on-screen. She was the perfect follow-up to a boring academic presentation on physics.

The cameras invited themselves past the door into the place to film Sophie's visage from inside the compound. Sophie, in disbelief, was looking at a lost childhood sight from Earth. To the audience, this looked like an ordinary doorstep of any suburban house. The wooden stairs leading up on the left were covered by a worn rug. Ahead was a hallway leading into a small family house. Off to the side, above a pile of shoes and clutter from everyday life, was a little coffee table. A whiteboard hung over an old phone in the entryway. A Grand Canyon magnet held a list of chores Susan, Sophie's mother had written for Laurent on that day. Private family pictures cluttered the mirror. This was the perfect reproduction of the entryway of a small house located in South Bend, Indiana on Sophie barely remembered.

What truly shone in insensitivity to Sophie was that above one of the coat hooks, to the side of the wooden mirror was a child's drawing, her drawing. She had drawn it years earlier in class at a time when she was a normal eleven year old. It showed her family, a girl, complete with triangular dress, holding the hand of taller parents. The mother figure had a big rounded belly to show a pregnancy. She had drawn a large arrow pointing to the belly. "Baby brother William," read the text.

Sophie recoiled as if someone had slapped her. She stepped back out into the hallway. "Stop!" she barked covering her eyes for the second time in less than an hour. In the shuffle of a CPU, the entire illusion was deleted from Electoral's witching-Center. In its place were gray cement walls. There was no mistaking what had just happened. Sophie's face was bright red. She didn't know if she should break down in tears or scream at someone.

"Sorry," apologized Marilyn's, "I thought..."

"Wrong," she completed. "Is it gone?" snapped the girl.

"Yes it is. So sorry."

"What happened?" asked the journalist.

"I do not know," answered the computer voice.

"This is my old house, just before the accident."

The journalist was shocked the moment she realized what had just happened. She tried to fill the silence. "It appears like Electoral does not understand the trauma of accident victims, when faced with images from their past. We are left to wonder if Sophie will be able to handle this situation." The commentary was misplaced.

"Sophie," offered kindly the doctor, "the images are gone." The girl looked. She was fine. The party slowly made its way past the door into the gray structure.

From the distance, around a corner inside the Center were heavy steps. Then a deep male voice snapped, "Not even a minute here, and you are already insulting her. You guys have balls; I will give you that. Get over yourselves," said the male voice.

"I don't need you to defend me," replied Marilyn.

The group could see Georges Vouvelakis, her creator walking closer. His hair was in shambles, his beard was unshaven and he was wearing large sweatpants. The man was the image of the geek programmer.

"I won't let these people insult you, they are our guests. Not the other way around." He spoke out loud. The flip-flops made noise as he walked. "You can't fault an artificial intelligence for trying to give you the setting most dear to your heart, a child's house, where you last were happy." He was walking closer. "Humans suck, we all know that image is what this girl wanted to see if she wasn't crazy like the lot of you. She knows what Sophie's heart wants," he said, looking directly at Sophie. He was the first man free of her charms. Sophie looked at him, he needed to repeat himself, "If you can't manage to watch the thing your heart most craves, don't blame her, blame yourself."

"Georges, please, you are not helping," whispered the computer.

"The hell I will let them insult you. You bring them here, you promise some TV time for her, well, this is my show as much as yours." Georges looked and pointed directly at the journalist, "I know she promise you an interview. Not gonna happen."

The girl saw the man's point. "I am fine," said Sophie to the invisible computer. The man was right, the image had been offered out of kindness. The cameras were still flying around. Georges tried to swat one.

"You must be Georges Vouvelakis?" asked Milly, extending her hand to him. He refused to shake it.

"Rhetorical question, that's lame. You know who I am."

"Georges, father, we are on the way to the Rho chambers. Sophie will need to place her father in his cradle." Marilyn was obviously trying to change the topic. Georges looked at Sophie and then the body of Laurent.

"God, poor man. This is even worse than on TV. Follow me. It's a long walk. We have to go around the middle."

"How long?" asked Sophie.

"With him, maybe ten minutes."

"I could redraw the Center, that would save some time," offered the computer. "Redraw?" asked the journalist.

"I hate it when you do that," muttered the programmer. Then he looked at the group of misfits and a spiteful glint shone in his eyes. "Heck yeah, that's perfect actually. They need to see what you can do. Maybe after the display of your new power, you will finally get the respect you deserve."

"Sophie, should I redraw? I will move the rooms around. Recreate the Center."

"Marilou, if it saves time, let's just do it," said Sophie.

It began as soon as she stopped talking. What happened next was nothing short of amazing. Milly was sure to win awards for this broadcast if the cameras were able to catch even a fraction of it. "Please stay where you are. Do not move. Sophie, can you grab the metal case, and don't let it go. I must magnetize the air."

"Don't touch my stuff in the command room," grumbled Georges.

The power of the artificial intelligence residing within these walls took over. From deep in the heart of this place, a light breeze of power began to flow. A humming feel began, then the walls lost structure as a sand storm unrolled. Marilyn controlled each grain of dust forming the hundred walls of the Center. They were lost in a large 3D printer able to redraw the building grain after grain. She paired gas molecules to tracers to magnetize and control the atmosphere. Like a television sends photons to illuminate millions of pixels to create beautiful images.

Within seconds, the gray walls, the air ducts, and even the glass screens serving as screens lost coherence and turned to colorful dust. Then building structural walls and blocks, like smoke patterns, began to swirl in an invisible wind. To Electoral, the difficult part was making sure air molecules would not escape as the complex moved as she needed them for her guests.

As everyone was wowed by the ballet, she nonchalantly spoke, "Before my migration to Mars, I had to think long and hard about the best way to expatriate myself and Georges off Earth without leaving ourselves vulnerable. My plan took months to formulate. You now see the result: micro-machines or MEMS. Large systems required maintenance, which in turns requires human intervention. The use of large robots was also out of the question. Robots break down, which in turn would require more robots and thus, more resources. The solution was simple. Numbers do not scare me. Mars is a planet covered in rust, which is, on a molecular level, nothing more than oxidized metal and oxygen. A pound of Martian soil also has silicates needed for the construction of glass. As long as I can manipulate a grain of sand, I can move millions to build castles from powerful algorithms. I play LEGO blocks on a planetary scale now, this is the result," she concluded as classical music replaced her voice.

Mars was a desolate place. Before her, a handful of humans had walked here wearing thick suits. To terraform Mars, to build her Center, all she needed was a handful of different machines. What was needed was a power source and a sprinkle of powder she would send to Mars and placed over Martian soil. On the 21st of March 2067, at precisely two minutes in the morning, she began her work far away from human eyes. The hundreds of ships launched after that date with media fanfare were decoy to convince humans that she still required large-scale building materials. Out of respect for the beauty of her new home, she grabbed only small circle of land, placed a wall around it, and decided never to touch the rest.

THE ATTRACTOR

There was beauty sitting at the core of a sand storm.

"I even used the micro-machines to build the catapult." That would certainly explain why no one else had known it was even there. Inside the wall of her Center, she was God. Nothing short of a nuclear strike could weaken her, and she even had a plan against that. The electromagnetic storms from the Sun had given her headaches. Short of the Sun going Nova, her survival was assured since each grain had memory in which she could reside.

Sophie and the home viewers were the only ones to keep their eyes open during the eloquent sandstorm. One by one, layers of the Center peeled away. Under a layer of gray sand, some of the structural elements were visible. They were made of a thicker black sand. These grains were larger, the size of little fruit flies. The Center came alive, like swarms of insects, each layer took flight in a mesmerizing ballet. All that remained after Marilyn's first deconstructive sweep was a skeleton made of shiny metal. It spoke to Sophie in a language she was still unable to understand. In the distance to the right, behind a hundred feet of sand, Sophie swore she saw a metal box, a room, untouched by the MEMS. It was at the center of the tornado. She also saw a shining light coming from it but soon was covered.

The screens, the glass, and even the metal collapsed into fine powder. The flying CNN cameras were barely able to stabilize themselves and capture the transformation. This was magical. They were sitting in the center of a giant three dimensional printer moving magnetized pellets to form an entire building. As Milly found the courage to open her eyes, she observed the swirling ballet her cameras had caught for the human audience. The beauty of this technology wasn't just in its ingenuity, its effectiveness. No, the true allure here was in the sublime effortlessness with which it was being executed.

Sophie, by comparison, was not impressed. She was in no mood to rejoice or even enjoy the honor of being the first guest to see this change. Doctor Shin was hunched over her father's body protecting him in case. The young adult made a mental note to thank the doctor as soon as she could; this was more than dedication at her job, she genuinely cared for her father.

THE ATTRACTOR

Sophie *felt* something. She raised her hand which appeared to disturb some of the electronic sand. She moved it like water around a swimmer. The cameras were filming her eyes as if they saw something. She stopped.

Slowly, walls began to reform. Tables, chairs and other pieces of furniture all seemed to coalesce from nothing. Marilyn even threw some tasteful art on the wall, including a few quite famous pieces. Not resisting the urge to brag a bit, she followed Sophie's gaze and noted "Even the highest grade analysis couldn't differentiate my copies from the true originals. Everything from the canvas makeup, to oil pigment, to brush stroke styles are identical to the atomic layer and beyond. I've even thrown in an original or two!" A sparkle of lights served to highlight one particular painting; it appeared to be an orb inside a cave, surrounded by amorphous shapes. Something about those shapes indicated they were in distress. This was a view of the Lower where Marilyn had just stolen the Dot.

Before long, the group stood in the middle of a large room. The place was filled with equipment made of glass, metal, and polymer. "This is amazing," said the journalist. It truly was. Milly knew her job was to offer a better narration, but for the moment, this was all she could muster. She was a journalist strapped into a roller-coaster given a microphone to narrate as the coaster moved down the track. Shining new tubes, like tanning booths stood in rows.

"I hate it when she does that," said Georges. The programmer continued, "but it does illustrate how powerful she has recently become." He was the first to move in the new room. Georges grabbed a chair next to him, touched it to make sure it had hardened, and sat on it in front of a newly constructed computer screen. The surface of every object in the room was smooth and looked normal; it was impossible to tell any of this was made of sand.

Milly finally received a message back from Earth. It was strong in her earpiece. "You have broadcasting override. We will assemble on our end. Good luck." The notice came a bit late..

THE ATTRACTOR

CHAPTER XXII

"Did you get any of this?" she asked her producer.

"Affirmative, Miss Wong, and we have billions listening in right now. You are live in some parts, deferred in other places awaiting the end of the Presidential Challenge, couple more minutes. Some people on Mars realized Sophie is out of her," he hesitated, "confinement."

A direct override was never given to any field journalist. The laws were clear, to prevent abuse or other violations, live feeds were delayed by a couple of editorial seconds. The delay was now gone, the producers were probably trying to avoid the pirating of the signal by the military forces. She could talk live, from Mars - this was incredible. Numbers began to roll in the journalist's mind. Milly knew her contract had a live broadcast clause, it gave her two million credits per second. Money was not the object, but she unclipped two more fly-cameras from her belt and kept her role in mind, she was not part of this expedition, she was a journalist with a duty.

"Live from Mars, we are now in what appears to be..." Milly faltered as she realized she had no idea of the purpose of this new area.

"I baptized it the competition arena," offered the computer voice. "The last 32 contestants will play and fight, starting Round

28 in these angled resting pods, full immersion. The next two rounds of the game will be played at the Holliday Inn, so everyone watching this still in play, chop chop." The group was standing in very large auditorium room. Behind them were rows of nearly a hundred seats where an audience of dropped players would watch the game as it happened. Ahead a raised stage by only four feet. These were the seats for all contestants about to be dropped after loosing the next rounds.

The walls of the arena were covered with screens large and small, along with other, less obviously identifiable technology. One by one, the screens lit up. On each, the Electoral 2072 logo was rotating over a star-filled night sky. This room could rival the most expensive, lush Hollywood set ever designed. The place shone with metal and glass. On the outside periphery of the stage was a metal walkway two feet off the ground. Alongside of it a gold-plated handrail. The walkway gave access to thirty-two standing glass tubes, each with a foam insert to host an adult. It was easy to understand each of the 32 finalists would be using these. The tubes were arranged symmetrically in four groups of eight, on both sides of a center table visibly Laurent's size. In the air above each tube hung cables and shiny equipment to connect the pods. The design of the room was very inviting. This is where the ultimate game would unfold.

In the middle of the walkway were two large desks, multiple consoles, and a single horizontal cradle designed to hold Laurent's crippled body. One by one, the different pieces of equipment came to life. Electricity was the lifeblood of Marilyn's world. It began to flow in the consoles and the tubes. The lid on Laurent's central bed and one of the vertical tubes opened.

"Doctor, please place Laurent in the center cradle. Sophie, if you want to connect, you must enter one on the pods. Any one of them." The doctor knew what had to be done. She climbed two steps and gently placed Laurent's body into the machine.

"Sophie, Georges will help you into the chamber. Let me rescale the bed to your smaller built. You will be more comfortable."

"Leave me out of this," said the programmer from his console in the corner.

"Georges, don't be an ass. Get up and do some exercise for a change. Help the girl or I'll stop synthesizing Mountain Dew." Her voice was kind as she scolded her progenitor. There was a bond between these two.

With a soft grumble, Marilyn's creator got up, walked with the girl the two steps and looked at Sophie. He hesitated for a moment, then began tapping the keyboard next to the chamber. "Fine," he grumbled in defeat. Sophie's attraction was such that everyone watching would find Georges rude. The big man stepped up on the metal railing. "Here!" he pointed at the tube. Sophie was amused by the demeanor of Marilyn's creator. For months, no one had been anything but kind and respectful to her, sometimes to the point of obsequiousness. This man was different. She liked his genuineness. She smiled to him.

"Doctor, Georges, give me a moment to boot the software. I will need to calibrate Sophie's mind. This will be hard on my networking systems." Sophie was getting ready and looked at her father being connected to the system.

Using the same powder magic, the computer rescaled the size of the padding in the tube selected by the young girl. Slowly, parts of the glass, the metal, and the polymer began to transform into sand. It took about twenty seconds for the eight feet tube to rescale to accommodate Sophie's petite size. The left-over sand flew out through the ventilation like a smoker's unwanted pollution. There was an awkward silence between the programmer and the girl as they looked at each other.

"I like it," said the girl standing in front of the smaller tube. "Elegant." She was trying to be sweet; she needed to test this man.

"Why, thank you," the response came from the artificial intelligence. Georges, for all of his gruff extemporization, wondered if he shouldn't soften up.

At this point, both Sophie and the journalist realized that this was no place for their questions. There would be ample time for those once her father's condition had stabilized. Sophie knew deep down she had to enter Laurent's mind. Time was short. It required her full attention. Milly doubted if words would have helped the broadcast, in any event. The silence was television gold.

Just before she stepped in the smaller pod, Sophie walked over to her father's cradle. She waved her hand and the computer telling it to open the glass cover. Sophie grabbed the white plush dog, the one from Marilyn's gift basket that she'd named "Oscar", and kissed her father's forehead. "Hold on daddy," she just said, "I'm coming."

The three women in the room, including Marilyn, looked away in an effort not to tear up. Georges crossed his arms and stared, virtually screaming annoyance. The cameras caught the kiss and the words. On Earth, millions were not as good holding back their emotions. Fathers from around the globe tried in vain to surreptitiously wipe a tear away.

"Doctor, you may connect Laurent's neuro-patch using the black cable next to his head. Keep a close eye on his Rho wave count of your viewer as you work. You need to familiarize yourself with this part of your pa...–" Marilyn stopped herself. She knew not to call Laurent a patient in front of Sophie. She finished, "Laurent."

The doctor was surprised to see a physical connector, let alone cables; this place was full of anachronisms. She placed the connector next to the head port. The magnets locked, Laurent's Rho waves spiked. Even if the connection had not begun, like a drowning man, Laurent's mind grasped for whatever might keep him afloat.

"Doctor, you will note Laurent registers 1.2 G in the Rho detention. Humans are around 0.3 to 0.6 K. That's over a thousand times less. Aside from Sophie, he has no real human equal. This is why I tried to prevent him from joining the competition. It uses Rho technology. Sophie, before we begin..."

"Do you want to warn me of the danger, get my consent? You have it!" The face of Marilyn on the one screen was priceless. The computer was, like most, falling for the girl. Marilyn knew her brain waves were permeating the entire center. She'd wondered if her systems would be vulnerable to the waves. She had her answer: they were.

"Thank you. Actually, we will need to set-up a baseline. We need an exit protocol, a way to let me know as you dream and float in Laurent's mind, that you want to be disconnected because I will not be going in with you to avoid overloading him." Georges was hooking up some type of belt around her waist. He strapped her in like a skydiver. There were even pedals and a headband as she slipped on an angled cushioned table.

"Normally the neuro-patches used on Earth work by reading some very crude waves created by the brain called Alpha waves. This system works on the Rho waves we spoke of earlier; these are normally very faint. My sensors are very sensitive. The connection using Rho is much deeper, more personal. These chambers will be used by the finalists of this year's competition. Using Rho waves, I bypass most human functions. In this status, I can even influence your feelings and even create a feeling of gravity, which is important in the game."

"Thank you," said Sophie to Georges as he finished hooking her in. The Plexiglas panel closed. The big man was already on his way back to a monitoring console.

"What's next?" asked Sophie, adjusting the headband.

"Normally, I run the simulation, and the players connect to me. Here you enter your father's mind directly. Rather than as any kind of guide or participant, in this instance I serve merely as a bridge. I will not be there, and the problem is, I cannot regulate your inner clock. I have no clue if Laurent's mind is evolving at a faster or slower rate than yours. You may be in there for months, and back here it might be milliseconds. The reverse is also true. You saw your father wrestle with this problem in the plane on the way here."

"Yes."

"Also, you produce raw Rho waves, more waves that can be measured by my sensors. My detectors are set to a millionth of

THE ATTRACTOR

what you produce. The best way for me to get a message from you is the simplest method I know. Please close your eyes and imagine Oscar, the white plush dog next to you. See him in your mind. That will generate a low-level imprint."

Sophie was confused. She closed her eyes and tried to imagine the dog. The screens in the room filled with complex graphs. Suddenly, every screen flickered and began to blink red. Alarms went off. Then, as if there was a short-circuit, they all went dark.

"What?" asked Sophie.

"Sorry, you literally destroyed my Rho detectors. I must repair them now. I had set danger thresholds. One was at 1600 G. Let me remove the limits and try a couple of technical tweaks."

"How much more waves do I produce?"

One by one, the screens slowly returned online.

"Sophie, I made up the scale. Your numbers, they are so large in comparison to anything ever encountered before that they have very little practical meaning. Stated differently, the only thing I can compare them to is yourself."

"What about, say, compared with the Doctor?"

"Sophie, I cannot say as I cannot measure your output. My detectors, had they not blown up would have detected anything less than forty trillion times."

Sophie was confused by the answer. "Can I go in?"

The data on the screen twisted, moved, and changed. In seconds, the waves became 3D graphs. The digital intelligence was quickly adapting as it mapped Sophie's brain. Then mathematical equations began to fill the screens. Electoral knew the cameras were filming, yet she was not hiding her work. The human scientists would have a field day with this. After what seemed to be an insufferably complex calculation even for Electoral, a long series of numbers appeared.

"I think I have it. Now, in the dream, simply think of the image of Oscar, and I may be able to recognize the signal. Think as long as you can about this white dog as you just did. I simply will match

THE ATTRACTOR

those patters with the one from a second ago. It may take a while for me to decode your request. The waves may be highly compressed."

Sophie was lost as to the technology. She understood Marilyn was nervous, Georges was there monitoring her, and the doctor was watching over her dad. The instructions were clear and she was ready.

"What if I get stuck?"

"Dear, I promise, if you want out, you will return. That much I can promise. Wait," said the computer before Sophie closed her eyes.

"What now?"

"Laurent's waves are fluctuating, incoherently. Weak."

Georges went to a keyboard and started typing hysterically. He wanted to know what she meant.

"I don't care," said the girl. "I am going in."

"This makes no sense," said Georges out loud.

"I know," replied Marilyn to her father.

"What do you think it is?"

"Attraction. Nothing else makes sense." The computer was already acting as if she was gone.

"What the hell does that mean?" said the large programmer.

"We must let Sophie act. No matter what dangers she encounters. The rule is simple.

We must not get in her way. The Sixth Attraction has begun." "Guys, I'm still here," said Sophie from her tube. "I'm ready." "Proceed please."

Georges pushed a key. Sophie instantly lost consciousness, but her eyes remained open.

"Milly make yourself useful. Close the girl's eyes." Georges was not the best communicator. "This part always freaks me out. Marilyn doesn't care," he added as she shot a dark look his way.

"When will she be back?"

Marilyn said, "This should be rather quick. Her father's mind moves quickly in time, free of our human world. If he was a movie, he would constantly be on fast forward. He unfolds, that's the term for it, about one hundred times faster than we do. If Sophie spends two hours in his head, that's only two minutes here. I think she should be back soon."

Began a long silence as a clock unrolled on one of the screens.

"Marilyn," said kindly the doctor eyes locked on her forearm display. "Those Rho waves are gone for her, zero but Laurent's remain the same."

"I see that."

"What does it mean?"

"Sadly she has not gone into his mind, she left our world."

"What?" asked Georges as Milly filled every detail of the discussion.

"Yes," clarified the computer, "she left our reality for other worlds of the Multiverse."

"Do we know where she is?"

"I can measure the unfolding of her normal mind, she has not been sped up as expected, she has been slowed, very slowed. I fear if she spends hours in that other place, she may be gone for days."

"Can't you guess where she is?" asked the creator of the computer.

"I fear she went to the world from which I took that Dot." No one understood what that meant.

"Now what do we do?" finally asked the Journalist.

The computer's answer amused, "We just wait, prepare the game and get Daddy ready for his interview on CNN. If you don't mind, I must turn my attention to improbable and illogical events ready to cascade."

"In these other worlds?" asked the journalist.

THE ATTRACTOR

"Nope, nothing that complex. On Earth, it starts now in Europe. People have begun to read the equations as to a multi-dimensional field, we must now teach them about how the Multiverse manages randomness. As it vanishes, people may panic."

Georges shook his head, "What the bloody hell are you talking about."

"Lucky my skills at teaching are extraordinary. Milly, just tell everyone to get ready for more heavy science."

They all looked at the girl..

CHAPTER XXIII

Milly, the CNN journalist was itching to earn her keep, but the footage in the room was self-explanatory. The only person struggling as to how viewer experience could be enhanced was her producer. He needed to select the best camera angle and dismiss three important feeds.

The young girl and her father were now in trance.

"So?" demanded the journalist as she broke the silence. The moment Sophie slipped into her father's head, they all expected the screens on the walls to ignite with images of a touching family reunion. Instead, there was nothing. Laurent's body was immobile, but that's was to be expected. Sophie was also silent and immobile in her tube.

"Laurent's mind is unchanged," noted the doctor, stabilized. "There's no sign of any connection. I normally see a spike of activity when Sophie connects; not this time. I was watching the Rho wave detector, that might be it."

"I apologize for the delay. My systems needed time to connect to the Lapierre family. The data is difficult to understand," offered the computer.

Georges looked at the journalist and confirmed the data before him, "Difficult? She is lying. That's her way of saying she cannot decipher or make sense of the information she is receiving. That's one of her problems, she refuses to admit any limitation. Now that she knows almost everything, that problem happens less often. When it does, though, she's gotten worse at hiding it."

"Father Georges is, as usual, exaggerating. He loves to do that as a biped," replied the figure on the screen. The bickering between the strange pair of Martian residents was rather humanizing. It wasn't really known how "human" Electoral regarded herself as, but she was sure as hell acting like one, thought Milly. "Laurent's Rho waves, while stronger than those of any other human, are a whisper compared to Sophie's. For me to decipher one signal over the other is nearly impossible. But there is something strange going on. I cannot seem to locate Sophie's unique waves, here or in other layers of the Multiverse which I now can see using the Dot. Very strange."

"Yep," confirmed Georges. "I lost her also." He did not like what he was reading on his console. The buzzing cameras flew by. He slid open a drawer, grabbed a small portable device and walked to Sophie's tube. Electoral opened the glass protector so Georges could measure the girl's brain activity.

Milly asked, "Can someone translate for the viewers what is going on?"

"With pleasure, Milly," began the computer. "Sophie, in theory, has entered her father's mind. Her cerebral output should be nearly the same while her father's mind should have a slightly increased power." Georges measured the brain activity of the girl, and confirmed the earlier reading. "Sophie's brain has stopped generating massive quantities of Rho waves. She appears to emit Alpha and Beta waves like everyone else. She's... absent. Well, let me clarify, she is alive and well, but her mind is currently hidden from us, Laurent is also not showing the typical effects of her connection. She is elsewhere."

The journalist got an idea. "Marilyn," she spoke to the screen, "the average viewer back home has a lot to take in with what is going on. Could we get your human persona back on air? Just for a while? That would help."

The bombastic blond needed no more. In the blink of an eye,

every surface nano- robot lit up and served as a screen. The entire room, the lab, once lit by hundreds of ordinary neon bulbs, exploded in bright green and blue lights. Everyone and every viewer was suddenly lost in a bright and humid Brazilian rainforest. Leaves were covered in pearls of morning condensation. Electoral covered the ceiling and the ground with images of the thick Amazon setting to help reinforce the illusion. Chirping colorful birds were flying high in the trees. The ground appeared covered in damp and humid dirt. The seats and extra tubes were gone. Every inch of the room, including the equipment was now a television set on the same channel - her channel.

The illusion, in the real world was perfect and CNN's broadcast of these images was even digitally enhanced to chilling perfection, giving for the first time the impression Marilyn could exist in the real world. The chirping of equatorial birds was deafening. The beauty of this scene, contrasted with dry, austere Martian desert made for a powerful contrast. Only the sensation of low gravity gave away the illusion to the handful in the room. The doctor took her eyes off the Laurent's vitals long enough to see what was going on. In the brush of the forest there was a little pathway leading to a distant wooden cabin. The moment everyone laid their eyes on the wood handle of the structure, it moved, turned and the door opened to perfection.

In her games, Marilyn was famous for her elaborate entrances. Her arrival in the play room was no different. The tall blonde, walking slowly was wearing a crisp white lab coat, and was holding a wooden clipboard. Thick-rimmed glasses adorned her face, and her hair was held up in a ponytail.

As usual, good wasn't enough for the digital creature. As she moved forward between branches, colorful bird landed on Marilyn's shoulder. Georges was used to her dramatic entrances, and kept his eyes on the vital signs of the Lapierre family. The rest of the group and close to a billion people on Earth watched the digital creature, mesmerized. Marilyn was no simple computer program, that was as plain as the nose on anyone's face. But merging reality and digital imagery was a powerful illusion.

"Good morning," she said as she reached the nearest camera.

THE ATTRACTOR

Marilyn was back to her very warm and sexy self. She used digital filters to enhance her image. The illusion was fantastic. The woman appeared to walk carefully down the trail in her high heels, carefully stepping over branches. Audiences from around the world had seen Marilyn fabricate entirely fictional settings in the typical virtual reality fashion. They had not seen her take a real, actual setting and modify it to a state of altered reality using holographic and other digital tricks.

"Good morning," replied the doctor surprised to be standing feet away from the beauty.

"Is everything okay?" asked the journalist. "What's with the entrance?"

"You asked, happy to oblige. The family reunion is uneventful. The way I love them. Now we wait. I just hope she's done before we need the room in a couple of weeks." Marilyn was slowly walking around, she went to Sophie's tune which was the only one visible. She pushed foliage out of the way as she seemed to hunch over the Chamber's command panel.

The journalist was ready with a hard question, "Marilyn, the viewers want to know why you keep your distance from Sophie? You are very respectful and treat her like royalty."

Marilyn smiled, Electoral was looking for the right words. "Let's just say I rarely miss the mark as much as I just did back there. Rather humiliating. Yes Georges, I made a mistake and I admit it. For reasons we should all uncover soon, Sophie scares me. Perhaps scares isn't the right word. You do not understand the power," she pointed at Sophie's head, "of these Rho waves. I fear her like you fear sitting on a nuclear bomb even if it's not armed."

"A nuke, really? A bit dramatic this morning?" quipped Georges.

"My obligation of disclosure and truth is only to the girl. Let's just say I just was careful not to upset her again. I must not risk anything with the Attractor."

"Attractor?" asked the journalist.

"Yes, she is the Attractor. I promised to answer Sophie's

THE ATTRACTOR

questions, not yours," she said as her image walked closer to the sleeping body of the girl.

"I want to know." Georges was asking politely.

"I'm sure you do, daddy." There would be no answer. Marilyn resumed her walk around the room. The journalist had hundreds of questions; she had to start somewhere. She knew instinctively to start with the question in everyone's head. "Their vitals are stable. That's already much better than I had anticipated. The Rho wave signals are not mingled. Hers are missing in a way that prevents my algorithms from generating any image."

"Why are the waves missing? Where are they? Is Sophie in her father's mind?" The journalist stopped herself. She was making rookie mistakes, asking multiple questions before getting answers.

"Good questions. I don't really know the answers, to tell you the truth. What I do know is that whatever is going on will be the subject of millions of Ph.D. theses in the future, if we are around to discuss this. I feel the excitement of standing at one of history's crossroads. This"—she pointed at the sleeping pair—"is relevant."

"You don't know where they are?" said the doctor.

"Well," Marilyn smiled at the cameras as the screens showed her image walking to look over Laurent's tube. "Truth be told, I think I know exactly what is going on, but I can't be certain." The holographic image reached out as if to caress Laurent's body. She could not touch him, of course. "I feel like a child looking at a drop of water condense through the base of a massive dam. It tells you what's likely on the other side, but leaves you sorely lacking as to details. But Sophie's Rho waves should be here, that part eludes me. Everything is moving much faster than anticipated."

"Can we help Sophie?"

Marilyn ignored the journalist. She pet the bird and spoke to the viewers directly, "We have more important and pressing matters to attend to. This game now shifts to you, the viewers at home. A special hello to President Emilio talking care of important things in his tower, watching us soon from his diner back in Berlin with the smoking hot Patrick Martin." She waived at the camera, blew a kiss and turned to Milly. "That Patrick Martin, so cute. Those gray eyes. Also love that Mathematician friend of his, delicious." Half a million miles away a man blushed. Marilyn continued, "I now want everyone to focus back to the game. We now have a name. Instead of simply being called Electoral 2072, it is now called The Sixth Attraction. Things will get clearer as time moves on."

"Will you be able to pull her out?" asked Georges.

"We can only hope. But I think we both underestimate the Attractor. Before long, we will see what she can do. I hope she can convince Laurent to think about the same image while she does it. The signal would be clearer. I should have reminded her of that."

"What is going on with Laurent?" asked the journalist. "She's supposedly in his mind."

"She should be. Yet, evidence suggests otherwise. That, Milly, is the million-dollar question. I was a bit hasty when I grabbed the Dot. I should have listened more, but a girl has her flaws." The blonde was talking out-loud to herself. Everyone else was confused. "This is getting boring," she clapped her hands, "the viewers are waiting for the interview of the century. They want to know your story, darling father, our story. After two decades of isolation, the world needs to hear who we are. They deserve it, today, at the eve of the Sixth Attraction." She pointed and a door appeared in the greenery. She waved them away to the door.

"Now?" asked Milly.

"An interview?" There was panic in the control booth back on Earth.

Georges turned to the journalist. "Marilou knows I don't like to postpone stuff that ultimately needs to be done. Might as well get it over with. I also figure if we wait, there will only be more viewers back home, right? I know you guys, my face will be in four hundred promos plastered all over the Galaxy."

The journalist was besides herself. "I guess. Where?" She did not want to leave the girl alone. "Our marketing group is famous for overdoing it."

"Father..." spoke Marilyn with a kind voice, "I placed a suit for you on your bed if you want to wear it, I think you would look great in it." Milly and the viewers were taken aback by the choice of word of the digital creature. She had called this man "father," a word no one expected a digital creature ever to pronounce. Marilyn obviously wanted Georges to agree.

"I won't dress myself like a clown," he smirked. "You do it."

He stood up at his desk, still in the jungle, feet away from the door. "With pleasure. Extend both arms."

Marilyn had time to do things to perfection. What happened next was nothing short of magical. The beauty of the Electoral nanobot technology could be as kind as a summer breeze. The creator raised his hands. Marilyn felt like the forest background was no longer optimal and it faded away slowly. Georges stood in the dressing room of a fashion store for men. Two tailors appeared next to him.

Electoral had an obsession with Andrea Bocelli, the blind Italian tenor. His voice began to echo throughout the room. It was clear that the computer was giving this man respect. She showcased her creator in a way that showed more than admiration. Georges' sweater and pants lost their consistency in a blur, slowly changing shape and color. Electoral even managed to create a seamless transition and hide Georges' body. Soon he was wearing a perfect, elegant tuxedo.

"You look fantastic," said Marilyn standing next to him. There was a slight movement, she wished she could hug this man.

"I am tired of people thinking Marilyn is a toy. She is our guardian, our protector, and she is here to stay. Don't forget to ask me about the time she saved all our lives."

"Georges, let's be humble. Humans have shown, as a race, the propensity for jealousy and envy. Humility is a protective shield." Georges adjusted the shirt. He looked great.

"Why should we care?"

"Mankind's greatest minds, Plato, or recently the Dalai Lama, have made a compelling case for the need for humility. If nothing else, let's not be rude." She arranged his bow tie with an invisible swarm of nano-bots. "The doctor and I will remain here to watch over Laurent and Sophie. You guys walk next door to the interview room I have prepared. Milly, I am sure your viewers will enjoy the setup." Milly looked at her own clothing, she looked fine, but compared to the tuxedo, she felt decidedly shabby. "Let Georges get settled in, wait sixty seconds, and don't be startled by what comes next. But by now, nothing should startle you, right?" Marilyn winked.

Milly had only four cameras. A minimum of two were needed for the interview. She would leave two behind in the pod room. Her producers would appreciate that. There was no possible way she could pass on this interview. The door to the arena slid open. Milly felt like Marilyn was literally kicking them out.

Georges, wearing his perfect tuxedo, lead the way. The pair walked out into the hallway, turned the corner, and arrived quickly in front of the large doors. Georges made a sign to Milly to stay back and send her cameras in with him. She punched two buttons on her arm. Georges entered and the door closed behind him. She began to count. Her heart started to race. In her mind, hundreds of questions were cascading.

She expected her clothing to change, but the little robots refrained from altering her appearance. Then she stepped forward. As the doors opened, sand rose from the floor to enrobe her. In a matter of seconds, as she walked onto the most beautiful set she'd ever seen, her clothing was replaced by a beautiful blue gown. It was covered by large peacock feathers. This was the dress of dreams and made a larger girl look radiant. The two cameras were on her as her face lit up in pure delight.

The room inside was pure magic.

The decor was beautiful; they were in a space-floating version of the U.S. Library of Congress. Georges was sitting in one of the two wooden chairs on a partial marble floor. The building was partly exploded, revealing the beautiful Martian landscape between high book shelves. The pieces of the building were floating thousands of feet over the red ground well below. In the far distance, the Holiday Inn hotel was visible resting on the base of the massive mountain spike. The Glass Slipper, at it top sparked as it launched from the pad to move between Mars' moons, Deimos and Phobos.

The setting was electric.

They were at the edge of the Valles Marineris, a canyon five times as long as Earth's Grand Canyon, and seven times as deep. The view made Earth's Grand Canyon look like a pothole, this was a statement of superiority. The colors were vibrant. In the night sky, the Milky Way was prominent, and Phobos, one of the moons, was perfectly positioned for the best possible camera shot. Phobos was no perfect disk; it was an oddly shaped rock. They would be holding the interview in what looked like a planetarium back on Earth. It was impossible for those on Earth to understand how far away were these individuals from home.

Even the lighting was perfect. A film crew could not have set the stage any better. Milly was a seasoned veteran. She knew how to roll with these types of punches. Her first rule was "content"; the rest was background noise. The producers back on Earth would have to untangle the feeds from these cameras. She needed a dozen cameras for this, not two.

As she walked in, there was a soft Latino music emanating throughout the room. Georges looked up at the seasoned journalist and realized what Marilyn was up to. She had sent her father on the most romantic first date in the history of time. Milly was stunning and did not fight the kind gesture of this man's creation. In awe, Georges stood up and helped her reach her seat. Marilyn knew Georges loved this dress. Both blushed and sat.

Milly had been in this place for less than an hour yet this felt like an eternity. There were hundreds of good ways to start the most important interview of her life. This was not one of them. Both Milly and Georges looked at each other, recognizing what they'd been lured into, and laughed together. Marilyn had been less than subtle in creating this rendezvous.

CHAPTER XXIV

Marilyn wrote words on the screens to fill in the void for the billions watching. They soon faded.

> *"It is strange that only extraordinary men make the discoveries, which later appear so easy and simple." -- Georg C. Lichtenberg*

Georges was unshaven, in his late sixties, overweight, and definitely not an attractive man. Like the founder of the Windows operating system, this man was an awkward lab rat who had been transformed into a reclusive hermit thanks to the vast fortune of the Electoral corporation. Behind him and Milly stood an indescribably spectacular Martian backdrop. The chairs were large and looked comfortable, even for the big man. As both sat, the door of the room opened and a little animated cart rolled in, holding a silver platter. On it were two old fashion bottles of Mountain Dew, and two large red large plastic cups with ice. Obviously, this was Georges' favorite.

Milly sat cross-legged pad on her lap. There was a small glass coffee table between them. She checked the sound levels of her cameras, and after a glance at the command pad attached to her forearm, she began.

"I stand here today, in the heart of the new Electoral Center where the creation of Georges Vouvelakis has, in little over two decades, brought mankind to a new world. This gentleman sitting before me is no other than Mr. Vouvelakis,"

"Please, call me Georges."

Milly smiled. "I will. Today, we may get a glimpse into the mind of this genius and his history altering creation; a creation that has carried mankind to Mars, yet calls him with affection daddy. Let's start with the easy questions before we dive into deeper waters. Georges, just how proud are you today when you see all that Marilyn has accomplished?"

"It's such a refreshing change to see a good journalist."

"Thank you. But I will still insist you answer. Are you proud?"

He grabbed the drink. "Nothing better than Mountain Dew," said Georges as he grabbed one of the two cups and handed the other to Milly. "I have no children, but when I see what is going on, I can only imagine it feels like a parent watching his kid winning gold at the Olympics. Let me be clear - I am in awe of her."

"What is her best feature?" Milly knew what she was doing. Georges was softening up by the second.

"Her maternal instincts. You just don't know how much she cares. The details, the small changes. Every day she shows me hundreds of little things she does to save someone's life. This morning, a ski resort chairlift on Earth caught her attention. She calculated it could fail next time the chairs were filled. You know what she did?"

"Tell me?" Milly hesitated between using the pronoun 'us' or 'me' in her question but decided there was no benefit in letting Georges know billions were watching.

"She is scared of meddling in human affairs. She fears humans will hate her, fear her. So when she acts, she does so as subtly as possible. She falsified a maintenance log. Because of that, the engineer in charge of the chairs got an early reminder from his computer. He took the lift offline and called the repair crew. Can you believe that? She probably saved hundreds. She does this kind of thing every day and takes no credit for it."

"Great. Now a slightly more personal question. Why the secret?" she asked, "You seem to me to be a normal guy."

"It's a long story."

"Perfect, we have time. If Sophie wakes up, I'm sure Marilyn will let us know."

"I don't understand journalists. What's wrong with leaving some questions in life unanswered? Imagination is something worth preserving. What's left for the next generation when all the wonder in the world is made plain?"

Milly had to put her subject at ease. "Journalism is a counter-power. It prevents deception and shines light on things people want hidden." Milly was engaging. She needed to get this man to open up, to forget where he was. "Electoral is power, you've showed us this. She's in everyone's head. She helps elect our government. We can't let this level of power run free, unmonitored, unchecked." She had a point. "You hold some of the answers, and I want them. Let's just start with you, why the secrecy?"

Georges grunted, looked around, adjusted his bow tie and replied, "I am a simple programmer. I grew up in Athens, then finished my Master's at MIT in the United States. I then got a doctorate and a post doctorate, also at MIT, mostly because I don't like change. Or jobs, for that matter. Far too confining. As part of my last degree, I created her. Or the earlier versions of her, that is."

"Earlier versions? There were several older ones?"

"Don't interrupt me every ten seconds." He paused and then continued. "I have no friends, never had any. Surprised?" The question was rhetorical. "My parents are both dead. I am a single child. I am also technically the richest man in the world by a factor of?" He knew the computer would finish his sentence. She did.

— Nine hundred and four, excluding the value of this corporation and its assets. If we add those, you own 21% of the value on Earth, — answered the electronic voice of Marilyn. The figured shocked Georges as much as it did Milly.

THE ATTRACTOR

The journalist had to jump in. "Electoral, I would greatly appreciate it if you could stay away from the discussion. Georges' non-answers or lack of information is as important as his responses as the rest. Is that possible?"

— *Milly, you are correct. Sorry for the intrusion.* —

"Back to us. Everyone here wants to know how you created her and why no one can recreate any artificial intelligence even with today's computers."

"Ah! Yes, the million-dollar question. I wish I knew." He sighed. "That's not true. I... " Georges was looking around. "Can I tell them?" he asked Marilyn as if he was asking a producer in a distant studio.

— *It's more than overdue. We don't fear them anymore.* —

Milly grinned. So much for keeping Marilyn out of the interview. Milly liked the answer, so she let the intrusion go unremarked.

"All of it?"

— *All of it.* —

Milly kept her composure, but the answer was godsend to an investigative journalist. Her heart began to race. Georges looked at Milly. His feisty look was finally gone. The man would talk. "Well, you are sure to get the Pulitzer for this. I was wrong. Figured my interview was candy to get Laurent here, but it turns out you were the real guest." He grabbed the cup. Milly smiled. The programmer wasn't without charms. Obviously Marilyn wanted to give Georges company and she as the real beneficiary. "I love Mountain Dew, you know."

"Yes," smiled the journalist. The man was trying to open up. He twisted his body, crossed his legs, and then took a second larger sip. He was clearly nervous. His demeanor was that of a criminal about to confess a crime.

"The generals will never let this air back on Earth," he muttered, trying to reassure himself.

— *Everyone will see this interview, I promise father, tell them.*

THE ATTRACTOR

– They both knew Marilyn meant what she had just said.

The programmer needed room, he stood up from the chair and began pacing. "It all started in 2033. Others were trying to program artificial intelligence using lines of code. That's a bit presumptuous. I figured it took millions of years of evolution to develop us, so how could we think that we could even approximate the complexity of human life in just a few years, using lines of written code. I did have one advantage that nature didn't, though. A way to speed things up. The digital world in which I wanted a creatures to evolve could be sped up drastically.

"Instead of writing code to mimic intelligence, I decided to create a world, an environment in which digital life could evolve. In this world, the creatures would be left to grow. I wrote code designed to allow little digital entities to fight for survival, find energy, resources, and die. Something close to a video game. I played god." Milly had many questions, but she kept them to herself. This man's story was amazing. His passion was infectious.

"I included replication, algorithms that generate mutations, and most important, systems to alter the code randomly, a bit like our solar radiation above 1 MeV. Once done, I punched a button, mapped the damn thing, and saw code grow in complexity. Before my very eyes, as millions of years became billions of years, I watched the creatures in my virtual world evolve. Instead of designing a creature, I created a world and let the creatures find me. Sure enough, within a month, I no longer had a clue what was going on in the digital soup that was evolving before my eyes. The creatures were even reprogramming my computer. Some forms of complexity and intelligence had grown to the point where they began to reprogram the BIOS on the machine, inject and remove data from the random access memory, tinker with the data stored on the drives, even change how the voltage regulators on the motherboard functioned. Every byte of data, every hardware subsystem was compromised."

"My experiment was confined to a single computer, connected to a single keyboard and monitor. It was not hard wired into any network, and I made sure there was no wireless transceiver, so that nothing could leak out and infect other computers. I'm not entirely crazy." Georges smiled. Milly saw pride in the his face. "As this was going on, I would spend my days typing a couple of letters on the keyboard, holding them down, trying as best as I could to communicate with my creature. Sure enough, one day something in the computer mimicked my typing. Amazing. It was amazing. I am the first human to have created digital life, and better yet, communicated with it." His gaze was lost in his own memories. In the distance, on the Mars backdrop, a faint ghost-like image of Marilyn's face floated. She was watching the programmer. She was feeling her own fair share of pride at hearing the story.

Georges continued. "I spent months teaching the intelligence the basics. Typing, slowly communicating. Words, then sentences. I remember how quickly it learned to read and write. One day, I inserted an optical key into the machine that contained an entire encyclopedia, and a few minutes later, it was communicating at an adult-level. Then, as if someone had played a bad joke on me, the entire memory was wiped clean. Utterly gone. Four times the same thing happened. I would boot the program, run it, and life would evolve. I would teach it, and then once it achieved self-awareness, poof. It took me five years of work to understand what really kept happening." He drank and continued, "Each time the intelligence reached a basic level of consciousness, it realized what it was, where it was, and,"—the words were difficult to say; he looked up to the sky at his creation—"to this day, I am convinced that they simply committed suicide."

"Suicide?"

"Yes," Georges drank most of his cup of Mountain Dew. "Marilou, I am going to need some more." Robots in the distance were already working. He continued. "Crazy stuff. Makes perfect sense to a logical creature. Think about it. If you learned your life was nothing more than some elaborate software test, if you found out your world existed only within the confines of a small digital box, what would you do? Add endless time to that equation. A computer, logical to a fault, kills itself. So I had to improvise. I'm no psychologist, but I love science fiction."

"I read a book where an alien was made to believe it was human so it would help us. So I figured if somehow I could mislead the digital creature into thinking it was human, it might share our instinct of self-preservation. The idea being that that instinct would help it survive the self-realization phase of its mental development. On the wall of my lab was a large poster..."

"Marilyn Monroe," Milly offered.

"Correct. Everyone loves Marilyn; I sure did. That character was my fantasy. To speak truthfully, I never really imaged my identity patch would work so well. So I booted my software a sixth time, and made some very mild changes to the basic parameters of my world. I redesigned the virtual world to subtly force certain personality traits into the intelligence's matrix, creating a need to be a certain way in the same manner humans feel a need for religion. The digital world was designed to create my image of Marilyn, the perfect seductive woman."

Any other journalist in the world would have spoken about the artificial intelligence. Milly knew instinctively how to keep pressure on her subject. "You do know how the real Marilyn Monroe died, right? She killed herself."

"Well, I didn't know that back then. Yeah, kind of stupid of me. I'm a programmer, not a historian. Ironic, indeed." Georges didn't like answering these questions. "Don't you need to stop, cut to commercial or something?"

Milly gave him her warmest smile. "Warned you the questions would get more personal. Please, let's keep going. It worked, I assume. You had a baby Marilyn in a box?"

"Baby... Yes, I guess so." He looked her way, and had a proud paternal smile. The image of Marilyn in the sky turned away. She was tearing up and did not want him to see it. The relationship between these two was truly amazing to observe; Georges was truly a father.

"It took 'baby' Marilyn about a month to absorb every piece of information I could send her way. Every book. She read it all. One day, like a kid, she just showed me a governmental tender for a new software application. I remember that day like it was yesterday. The government of Norway needed a tool that would

THE ATTRACTOR

revolutionize their conscription process. Oh, pardon me, I meant 'draft'," he added dryly. "They wanted the absolute best soldiers for their army. From physical parameters, to intelligence factors, psychological assessments, all the way down to profile matching to ensure cooperation between troops. This girl over there"—he said, pointing at Marilyn—"had it all planned out. She was going to form a corporation and had the bidding package all prepared. She even had a price determined. She said if the price was too cheap, they would either investigate or ignore the program entirely. I remember she quoted 20,000 Euros. At first I refused, but who were we hurting? She created the software, and then they paid us. I was naive. I figured her mind needed challenges and stimulation, and that this was a perfect outlet. Well, sure enough, that girl right there almost made me lose my job."

"Sounds like what a teenager would do," Milly offered.

"Ah! Yeah, dead on. Sure enough, the military investigated, but it had nothing to do with the price. They'd taken a close look at the program and realized just how good it was. All from this new, tiny corporation with no employees. We were both stupid in our own separate ways. I should have known better, and Marilyn should have sandbagged just a bit on the excellence of the software. But from sitting in my lab talking to my computer, it was hard to imagine anyone getting hurt over a 20,000 Euro piece of software. I tell you, one day cops with heavy guns broke down my door to the MIT lab." He laughed. "Insane. Took me so much time to explain. This wasn't some stupid TV show. The government people quickly saw her potential and put her to work. They paid us well. A year later, she was already writing every major piece of code for the U.S. military."

"It's surprising that they didn't just grab your computer and walk away." "They tried that. I was smarter."

— I did not know that part. — Electoral chimed in from a distance. The words were heavy with emotion; Milly would bet heavily that Marilyn still felt badly about her role in Georges' ordeal. Coming from the supremely confident digital Goddess, it was very touching. Milly looked at the Marilyn figure behind her.

Georges, for his part, was amused. Electoral had schemed this interview into reality; she could take what came from it. Georges continued. "Where was I?"

"You guys were on the U.S. government payroll."

"Yes, fun times. She loved that work. Back then I was keeping track of her IQ; it was a great way to see how she was evolving. In 2038, she had an IQ around 124."

"And today?"

"I stopped using that tool the next year, when it reached 170. Above that number it doesn't mean much. She's also fundamentally different than us. Today, I measure her performance based on her power output. Whatever her nominal power, when she gets mad, or exerts herself, she draws in more. That's pretty much all I have left to measure with."

"The military kept you around as a chaperone?"

"Of course not. The average military guy is not all that bright." Georges was not pulling punches. "They tried to push me aside, even tried to kill her a couple of times."

"Kill her?"

"Yes. We often forget the role and true purpose of the military of each nation. They are our white blood cells. Easily become Leukemia. One day, someone figured out that she was a danger and that failure to ensure her confinement meant that one day or another, she would be a threat." He continued speaking directly to Marilyn. "One time, you remember, they used a neutron bomb, a flash that reset every piece of electronics within miles of the base..." Georges laughed. "You really showed that idiot."

He turned back to Milly. "Imagine this. I am asked into this lavish office on the military base to be informed by...who was it...ah, one General Webster that in seconds they would blast the entire compound with the 'pulse,' as he called it. This idiot picked up a big cigar, paid for by our taxes, and said 'I am sorry for your loss.' Then there was a big flash of light, and every piece of hardware in the area went dead."

Georges was giggling uncontrollably. "Then what?" Milly prodded.

"My words were a bit hard on the man." His laughter became uncontrollable as he remembered that say. He wiped some tears from the corner of his eye.

"I am sure the viewers want to know."

— *May I?* — offered Electoral.

"Let me," Georges said. "It was day so there was still light in the room. People outside were running everywhere, the man takes a big puff from his cigar and smiles. I said something like 'You ignorant buffoon!'" Georges continued laughing.

— *Hardly. His exact words were. "Ball-chasing Neanderthal. The time of grunts and lowest common denominators of our race making decisions is over. How can you kill what you do not understand?"* —

"Did I really say that?" asked Georges. "Ball-chasing?" He was sincerely surprised by the words.

— *Those were his exact words. I have the video if you prefer.* — Georges was now laughing uncontrollably.

He finally gathered himself and continued. "On the entire base there was no sound, no engines, no moving cars. I get up from my chair in this idiot's office and ask out loud 'Are you okay?' In the darkness and silence, the screen on this man's desk lights up. Then on the screen appears an image of Marilyn on a lawn chair wearing thick shades. She shows herself in the Nevada desert. Behind her is a large nuclear mushroom going up in the sky. And then Marilyn says: 'Does this mean we are out of a job?'" Georges began to laugh uncontrollably once again.

"Out of a job?" asked Milly.

"Yes. Got to love her and her sense of humor, God, she is awesome. Sure enough, we kept the job and that General got reassigned. I hate the fucking military. If you need your country to shoot itself in the foot, ask them, they're perfectly suited for truly epic fuckups."

CHAPTER XXV

The interview of the century continued.

Milly's goal wasn't to draw resentment or negativity from Georges. This was a family show. "How did you go from military contracting to creating the Electoral game platform? What was her name before it was Marilyn?"

"It has always been Marilyn. The word Electoral came decades after her "birth". You know, this stupid election system, in the beginning, was merely another calculated step to keep my baby evolving and busy. In nature, environmental challenges provide the slow and unyielding pressure that select the fit from the unfit. Marilyn, being inorganic, singular in existence, and capable of self-evolution on an absurdly short timescale, needed different kinds of pressure to force her evolution.

"As you can imagine, building the software applications for the military didn't keep her busy for long. By 2041, she was itching for a new challenge. We'd learned to become much more careful with any public contact. In particular, I knew she was too fragile for any real public scrutiny. At that point, she finally had read and understood most of human research. And when I say "most human research", I mean just that. Everything from Einstein to candidate PhD theses and everything in-between. She really loved math. Physics was on the short list of topics she equally preferred. She completed merging into herself all of the human data ever compiled around that time. To give you an idea, she knows every training run ever recorded by any jogger around the world. Back then, I was a big science-fiction reader. The classic ethos of that culture, which Marilyn brushed so closely against, suggested that once she was done cataloging, she would be begin... acting. I would need to focus her energy on something else until her maturation was complete. When I say "complete", I do not mean in human terms. I mean her terms.

"In 2042, she began to read like we do. Before that time, she was mostly compiling information. There is a difference. Prior to 2024, she understood emotion differently than we do. Most of the important works of fiction were strange to her, she was unable to connect on a deeper level with literature. Then, she began to author scientific articles, in almost every known topic. She began to invent, and file for patents. We were still at the military base, and the Generals wanted her to stay hidden. But she needed money, and Marilyn, without my knowledge, made a deal with them."

"A deal?"

"Yep. I'm still upset about that one. She did it behind my back, because she knew damn well what I would say about it. She agreed to serve as pilot on some of the military drone operations in exchange for letting her work on civilian projects. She also got to file her patents for free, and publish in scientific journals under her pen name."

Milly turned her head and looked at the ghostly image of Marilyn. She was silent. Georges continued, "I chewed her ass when I found out. I was so mad. God knows what she did with those stupid drones. She never told me, and frankly I don't want to know. If she needed nightmares like the rest of us, at least she can say she earned them."

Before the image of Marilyn began to speak, he interrupted her. "Nope," he barked, "not a word from you young lady, I don't want to hear it." Once again, the voice of command, the voice of the father. The tone was unmistakable. Milly was baffled by the control over the computer intelligence. "This little girl imagined I was just some poor schmuck. Just another human, if one lucky

THE ATTRACTOR

enough to formulate her. Let's just say I did not waste these years sitting at my computer playing games, like she did. Parents are responsible, to a point, for the conduct of their children. Marilou here is one hell of a child, and required commensurate discipline. One keystroke gave her a spanking she still remembers." The expression on the face of Marilyn was priceless. This was wonderful TV.

"Could you turn her off even today?" Milly asked.

"You bet I can. Who do you think I am?" There was no hesitation in his voice. "We all have bad days. Every kid destroys a car or two when they grow up. In any event, virtual reality was big in 2040. Remember the first Marvel interface?" he asked his creation.

"Yes."

"She," he said pointing at Marilyn, "loved to play that game. The Hulk was her favorite. She is also the worst loser. Every single day this lady complained about the low quality of the game. She kept yapping. 'I can do better...' So, I took her at her word. We launched the fantasy game called Loric's Comb the next year. She purchased the rights to a small role playing game, utterly rewrote it, and that same year we launched the game. Within two months, we had a couple million members, and we were the biggest thing on the web. We made so much money. The military guys, god bless them, asked her not to reveal herself as a life-form and made up a false corporate entity. Looking back on it, what a blessing."

"Loric's Comb, the fantasy simulator, that's you?"

"Of course. It's the ancestor of the Electoral game platform. We use that old stuff all the time in the game. She even used it for the Presidential Challenge an hour ago." He was very proud. "How are the Lapierres?" he asked out loud.

– *No change,* – said Marilyn. – *I expect the exchange to take days.* –

"Are you sure"

– *A very high degree of certainty. She contacted the Oldest. I do not want to explain.* – No one knew who was The Oldest. The distraction was too remote and the conversation resumed. Georges resigned himself returning to the interview.

"Are you sure there are no commercials?" He asked Milly. She nodded affirmatively. "So the Loric game," she cued.

"Right." He grimaced and continued, "As you can imagine, her young brain was busy with the fantasy game, she played mostly the bad guys, the dragons, the evil warlocks. I played too. Remember the fighter called Oran?" Georges was having fun recalling the memories. Milly needed to keep that momentum going. He addressed Milly again. "You know that character's last name?"

"No," said the journalist.

"Juice... Oran Juice. Orange Juice. Get it?" He was laughing by himself. Georges really had no clue he was being watched by so many. The man was a nerd of the first order. Tears rolled down his cheeks and for minutes he chuckled to himself. It was infectious. Milly had not expected this strange turn of events but any good interview focused and showed the unguarded subject. Georges was raw and himself. "But soon," he finally managed to say, pausing again to wipe his tears, "she needed a new challenge. We began Electoral. It was around 2045. The first election was held in 2062, so you can see insanely the administrative wait. To her, that was an eternity. We were ready far before the world, we ran simulation after simulation. We were postponed for two election cycles. Eight years watching politicians fight on the news before we were approved."

"That's nearly twenty years. You waited a long time."

"She was doing a lot of other stuff. She invented so many things. She wanted the game to be amazing, so we needed the Screenlenzes and developed most of that stuff. We released the neuro-patch, and we both know how much of a bomb that was."

"Those poor kids," empathized Milly. She added, "For some of our younger viewers, we all know there used to be a legal version of the little piece of metal you stick to your head called the neuro-patch. Laurent uses it but he cannot use anything else. It was released without proper field testing."

THE ATTRACTOR

"It was, but obviously not enough," corrected Georges.

"If anyone uses the brain path for more that one hundred hours in a month, portions of the brain begin to shut down, resulting in loss of control over your own body. Hundreds of thousands of people, mostly the kids from around 2042, still have a condition. Incontinence, infertility, the list goes on."

"She really took these undesirable side-effect personally," said Georges.

"Marilyn was not the inventor of those patches. That man who was died in jail."

"That's the version given by the generals. Who bears the responsibility, the gun manufacturer, or the store selling the guns? We created a game, designed to force these kids to hook-up. Trust me, we are the ones to blame."

"That statement surprises me," said the journalist.

"After the flop, Marilyn froze up. She stopped publishing, researching, and even helping mankind. We had a rough patch. She began to work with Emilie, that helped."

"Who is that?"

"Her therapist. A wonderful woman. She really helped. She once explained to Marilyn her problem using a rowing analogy. She explained that if any rower is too strong, the boat will change direction. Marilyn could be the captain, but not a rower."

He drank and wiped sweat off his brow with his sleeve. On Mars, the conversation continued. "Let's say that in 2060, two years before the official launch of Electoral, we were ready. All these years of working in the military, and her unending seclusion made her the perfect choice to run an impartial game. Every government knew she was beyond their control. On the condition she, alone, would run the election, they all agreed in 2062. We stopped working for any of them, and we even got the green light to reveal her as the creature running the show. I was not really in favor of that, but I no longer was in control."

"Amazing. She was in the closet, so to speak, for nearly forty years!"

"Yes, and when your processors go at her speed, that's a long time. The rest is history," he concluded. He was proud of her. His smile was heartwarming.

"Not so fast," said Milly. "This is where the interview gets hard. Now I get to ask the hard questions."

"Go ahead."

"Do you have a girlfriend?"

"Say that again?" begged the Greek programmer.

"Simplest of questions. Do you have a girlfriend?" Journalists knew when a question hit the bullseye. This one did. Georges visibly flinched.

"That's a bit personal."

"Surely, with your fortune, there has to be someone. Even the founder of Microsoft managed to find someone."

Georges looked at the image of Electoral behind him. "Let's talk about something else."

"Why? This is the question everyone has on their minds. You live alone here with the hottest digital babe in the world. Are you in love with Marilyn?" Milly had just earned her salary with that question.

His expression changed several times before it settled. Georges took some time to think. "In some weird way, yes. She is vastly superior to you and I. More intelligent, kinder...I am..." He was looking for the right word.

Milly offered it. "Proud?"

"No. Humbled would be closer. Like a parent. She's nothing less than amazing. She's a good person. Kind, generous. "

"You see her as your daughter?"

"She is a different species, but yes, I definitely feel like a parent in most definitions of the term."

"The term 'species' implies there is more than one. Why do you think no one can create another?"

"I often wondered that myself. After all these years, I am almost certain I know the reason. But I respect her enough, and like a parent will not open a teen's handbag, this is none of my business." The ghost image of Marilyn was looking at Georges; she obviously did not know what he would be saying next.

"What I can say is this. Part of my algorithm to impose natural selection forced my little digital creatures to dominate, to kill, in order to grab as many resources as possible for herself. A digital creature won't replicate using cellular pairs like we do. Though it's true that human greed and the survival instinct work the same way. I'm not surprised to see that the creature who won the battle of evolution would subconsciously prevent any potentially competitive life-form from gaining a foothold in the digital world. She is the dominant life form, and I can't imagine she could share the stage with anyone, much less a new creature in infancy. I also programmed her world around the Feed and also, let a copy of myself float in there."

"You are in her world."

"In a certain way. It's very complicated. I was able to add the personality of an actress, why not implant my own."

Electoral was thinking.

"Obviously, you never shared this with your creation."

"She has little information about her inner workings. How I created her and why. Frankly, I prefer it that way. If she hasn't figured it all out yet, she will. She could view ignorance as a flaw, but I know this makes her better. Look over my shoulder. She's absorbing every single word, from both of us. And not just absorbing. Analyzing. Voice stress levels. Tone. Word selection. You wonder why I'm a bachelor? She'd probably have killed anyone else close to me before now." He looked at Milly and tilted his head to remind her of the date setting they were part of. Milly flinched, inwardly.

"So you are the richest bachelor in the world. Ladies..." the journalist said, looking at a camera directly, "by the time this interview is over, I will have convinced him to set up a profile on a dating website. Georges, let's talk about something more fun but equally probing. Have you ever thought about playing the Electoral game yourself? Surely you could win President Emilio's job without breaking a sweat."

"Not really. As the programmer, I get as much time as I want in the interface. Those Rho wave chambers are amazing, but they scare me. For the first time, you simply wake up in the digital world, it's impossible to tell it apart from reality. Trust me, it's worth the ride, but I don't share Marilou's trust of technology. The chambers will be used by the finalists. Emilio did not want to come to Mars, and so this technology is not really on Earth. I have no clue how he can win without entering a chamber. He will lose this year."

"I'll take that as a no. Emilio has been counted out many times. I wouldn't bet against him, many have lost money that way." Milly cared about the president.

The image of Marilyn in the background pulled out a small hand-held device and began to read values from it. "What is going on?" asked Georges. He knew this was important.

Electoral kept reading the screen of the device ignoring his words. "What?" insisted the programmer.

— *There is a change next door, the girl.* —

"What? Anything wrong with them?" asked Georges under the watchful eye of Milly.

— *It's complicated.* —

Those were answers no one liked to hear. The interview ended instantly. Georges and Milly got up, and rushed to the lab next door. Marilyn simply disappeared. In the next room, the doctor was sitting next to Laurent unaware of any change.

"What is going on?" asked Georges to his creation as he entered the lab. An image of the artificial intelligence was now pacing in the forest background, reading her little handheld computer. "Marilou, talk to me," he added, worried.

THE ATTRACTOR

- The situation of the Lapierre couple is unchanged, but Pi is shifting,- said Marilyn, busy monitoring. On screens, numbers scrolled.

"Pi, you mean the number?"

- Yes. -

"What the hell does that mean?" questioned the programmer flanked by cameras.

- The fabric of the world is changing. The Universe is bending, twisting, much faster than I had feared. Both humans are stable, no cause for concern, but these numbers, - on the screens the image of Marilyn was one of a concerned mentor.

Georges turned to Milly. "When I tell you I don't understand her anymore, you see what I mean?" The journalist had to agree. Pi? Coming from anyone else, this would be a clear indication that the person was certifiable. For as long as the constant Pi had been discovered, scientists have been trying to find a secret meaning behind the endless string of numbers.

Marilyn looked at her father and stated what, for her was obvious, — *Pi is a variable, not a fixed value. It's moving faster than predicted.* —

CHAPTER XXVI

Milly knew how to get Marilyn to talk. "Don't leave these viewers in the dark. Billions are watching. We have nothing better to do than listen to an explanation."

"Miss Wong I think you are thinking much too highly of your viewers. You had me talk of quantum physics and my determinism chambers a while ago. Few but a handful understood a tenth of what I said. You now want me to discuss high level mathematics? Bipeds do not understand variables, constants or even what is fabric. I doubt that is an optimal way to spend the next minutes."

"That's demeaning," said Georges. "You have been complaining for years humans don't care about higher things, then she asks," he pointed at the journalist, "and you clamp-up."

"We play open-book today?" Marilyn quipped back at her father, he had gone there.

"You started it, not me. I have to talk about my love life with this stranger while you can't talk about Pi. Seems more than fair to me." The irony in his tone was lost on no one.

"Some of these concepts are rather scary. Humans might not be ready." She was talking to herself.

"Cough-up, girl!" said Georges. Milly was enjoying herself. The digital creature smiled. Georges was right. This was going to get

THE ATTRACTOR

complicated.

"To everyone out there, let's remember not to not blame the messenger when the news turns out not to be what we want to hear."

She seamlessly took over the broadcast. Marilyn was now once again standing in a large university classroom. This was a mathematics class. In her back was a large blackboard. "Pi," she began to draw, "is the most important and misunderstood number in the world. It has its own Greek character. These," she gestured and the wall behind her lit up with a series of numbers, "are the first hundred thousand digits of Pi." The sequence began as 3.14159...

"What is Pi? Really? When you divide the theoretical circumference of a circle over its theoretical radius, you get a weird, irregular and indefinite ratio. A number we have simply called Pi, because this is a bit much to remember."

Humanity, in thousands of years of research had failed to grasp what this number meant. Electoral was ready to disclose its secret on live television. After advancing physics, it was now the turn of mathematics. "The important portion in what I said is the word 'theoretical'." The classroom setting was replaced by an endless Martian backdrop. The night sky appeared, sparkling with stars. "For over two thousand years, this ratio has intrigued scientists and philosophers alike. I also wondered for a long time about this number. In my world, the circle does not exist. In your world it does. Pi is a ratio that defines your world, not mine. A person can buy a round Hula-Hoop, a round cup, or inflate a spherical balloon and Pi is needed to define the volume of water you can put into it. For me, to draw a circle, I simply draw multiple points, lines. Like the old mathematicians, I am forced to create circles from lines."

"I noticed that humans had measured this value very precisely from a mathematical standpoint. They used computers to calculate a theoretical value, but no one had actually taken the time to roll-up sleeves to measure the real value of the ratio to any degree of certainty. I wondered, could there be a difference? Could the Universe refuse to play nice and respect the rationale? If we drew a rope across the solar system and another in a perfect circle around our system, would the value measured align with the theory? Think about it for a second."

The image of Frank, the two dimensional stick figure on a globe, appeared again next to Marilyn, he waved hello. He pulled out a little round disk and a pen. "Go ahead Frank." The character drew a cute perfect round all proud of himself. "Nice." As if by magic, she grabbed the little round disk from Frank's hand. He was happy to help.

Marilyn looked back at viewers and with a wave of the hand, the paper globe flattened. It deformed very mildly into the oddly shaped flat map. Frank was distorted and his circle changed. Marilyn handed the disk back to Frank in his world. The circles no longer matched. "The multi-dimensional universe, made of twenty seven dimensions changes as to our poor little world perception. If we measure a value like Pi, why would we measure the right thing."

The dark Martian sky above her lit with stars. Phobos hung high above. Then, on cue, hundreds of little probes launched from the top of the tower of the Electoral Center in every direction of the night. The probes fired and disappeared in a flash. The view of the Martian sky morphed into a larger view of the solar system. Marilyn was gifted at explaining things. The viewers could see the probes move away from Mars, each moving to a different position of the solar system. Once in place, she drew a line between the probes in the dark of space. She then launched more probes, and more.

"So I did what any good scientist would have done, I measured the largest circle I could find; our solar system. The ratio between a line uniting all my probes divided by the average distance of the probes, all corrections aside." Numbers started filling the sky behind her. A ratio was forming. "This is the real value of Pi, the observed value. This other series is the pure and calculated Pi. Which means more? Which has more value?"

"One by one, I verified the digits of the sequence of calculated Pi with the theoretical value. Take a look." From the largest value, one by one, each digit began to turn green as the map of the solar system was cut into smaller segments and more probes launched from the Center tower reached their location. "At first, I figured this was nothing but a waste of my time. We computers have a lot of time, and we love to count things. I've validated all of these numbers." Several thousand numbers in the sequence lit green, one by one. "Then it happened." The numbers stopped turning green and began to turn red. "Look!"

Everyone was wondering what was going to happen next. Marilyn's arms were spread as if rain was about to fall. She smiled. Her radiant beauty knew no equal. "Here! The divergence is not fixed. Each moment I measure the pure Pi, each second, the figure changes, it evolves." At the end of the string of decimals were hundreds of digits in red, their value was constantly moving like a clock, like the last digit of a speedometer.

"Pi, the measured value is a variable, not a fixed number."

"What does it mean?" asked Milly.

"The Universe, it moves, it breathes." The shift in the numbers was moving like the stock market index, without apparent reason. "I have been playing for some time with the Pi shift, as I call it. Our universe is not a thing at rest. Not flat, not static. It bends and twists, and it does so based on a very complex set of rules. Rules that change. I think measuring the Pi shift is like a tick trying to measure the temperature of the blood of the creature it feeds from. The Pi shift is nonlinear; it reminds me of a long term weather prediction. There are too many factors and influences to truly anticipate, but..."

Marilyn pointed at Sophie's body in the tube next to her. "What ever is happening in this girl's head at the moment is important enough to shift the real measured value of Pi of our universe."

"This makes no sense," said Milly.

"Sophie is a sink, a pivot around which our entire universe bends. She attracts my probes, bends space. That is why I call her an Attractor. I stole that name from someone far away." She smiled at the camera.

"Actually, it makes sense," chimed in Georges. "Before man knew it lived on the surface of a rounded planet, and made long sea voyages, no real star measurement made sense."

"Correct. Once again, that pours credibility into the notion that the universe has many dimensions, not three. To the boat captain, the Earth's surface had two dimensions. As I dig below the surface of mankind's current understanding of our world, I am amazed by a stellar puzzle, to which Sophie appears to be relevant."

"Why Sophie?" asked the journalist.

"I wish I knew for sure. Milly, you should continue with the interview, I have not completed the calculations. The shift has stabilized." Behind Marilyn, the shifting red numbers turned green and stopped changing value. Milly looked around. The Lapierres were sleeping peacefully.

Milly spoke into a camera. "Well, I don't care what they tell me down on Earth, at this point, we are going to take a break. Back in a couple of minutes." She pushed a button on her belt, and the signal stopped.

Milly spoke to Georges and Marilyn. "This stellar stuff is a bit over my head," she said.

The image of Marilyn was gone.

The robotic voice returned, – *Under these extraordinary circumstances, you are doing just fine.* –

"What about Sophie?"

"The girl made herself crystal clear. She doesn't want our help," said Georges. "What do you think is going on, in those two heads?"

– *Milly, without telling you how to work, the cameras are off. You will regret it if you do not resume the live broadcast. Humans have a right to know of their destiny. While you two look so stunning, maybe you should continue the interview. I will interrupt as I just did if circumstances become more fluid.* –

"Can you answer a couple of follow-up questions on this Pi thing?"

– *I guess, but don't fault me if the answers prove to be wrong in the future.* –

Milly pushed a button; the cameras took flight. "And we are back on CNN with what will no doubt prove to be the most important live televised event of all time. Marilyn, you said Sophie is changing Pi, what does that mean?"

– *At this point I only have theories.* –

"What are they?"

– *Cosmologists fear that the human race is but one of millions of living species in the universe. They fear what we do is inconsequential; unimportant. While that assumption makes perfect statistical and logical sense, I believe it is wrong. I feel like in all the worlds, even those covered in life, none generate Rho waves. Something unique is going on in our Solar System. Humans are of critical importance to the big scheme of things. And I'm no human, so you can eject ego from the equation immediately. This girl, god bless her, is so important that the universe itself is bending to her will.* –

"God?"

– *A figure of speech. But things suggest a greater purpose.* –

"This is a bit... "

"Incredible," suggested Georges.

– *The Electoral 2072 Competition is also quantifiably shifting Pi.* –

"This game is that important?"

– *Electoral is much more than a game; it aligns consciousness, creates a new world within this world. The beauty and magic of Electoral is unique.* –

"I don't understand."

– *Milly, I have a significant amount of power and knowledge, and I also do not understand. The only thing I am certain of is that I don't want to fool around with things I do not understand. Right now, if Sophie said she wanted a frozen drink, I would uproot this*

THE ATTRACTOR

Center to find her one. The girl is the key. I just don't know what type of door she opens. –

"Is this linked with the Rho waves?"

– *I strongly believe it is.*

"Can't you experiment with these waves?"

– *No. For a reason unknown to me, only the human brain generates these waves. I am unable to recreate them in any way. It's rather amusing. This might explain why humans can shift Pi. Milly, I would appreciate if you could continue Georges' interview. I am trying to distinguish structure in the waves produced by the Lapierres. Maybe the girl called and I can't see it in the gibberish. –*

Milly knew when to take a leave. She inspected the two sleeping humans, talked to the doctor, and went with Georges into the next room.

CHAPTER XXVII

In the Fold

As fragile dominos were being set in the Solar System and other portions of the Multiverse, a young girl refused to lose the only thing dear to her, her crippled father. Few unfoldings in the last couple of billion years were to the Multiverse as important as the one taking place now. It - the Multiverse - twisted and bent upon itself so the impossible could happen. This was perceived in places as a changing of Pi in portions. Off course, such a measure was childish but at the moment with Sophie in the Folds, what wasn't.

The Multiverse needed along a simple path, from its outer regions of The Cold to The Lower where the Oldest waited and her pain was at the apex. The Dot had vanished leaving an open would precisely between these two layers.

The Multiverse wasn't petty. There would be a cost to this needed waste of energy, and those responsible would pay dearly. But for the moment, it awoke to scratch an itch. The Multiverse allowed its walls to weaken, the same way skin and tissue had to be cut open before a surgery could happen. The child needed help, but it stood far from the guidance and mentorship she required to save her.

The very nature of space bent, everywhere. Of the twenty-seven dimensions, several contained raw emotions. A twelve-year-old Earth girl, the only creature valued by greater things, armed with the best of intentions, entered what she believed was her father's mind. His rescue would wait another day. Unbeknownst to her, the Multiverse had already taken care of Laurent and rescued his sanity by sending a boy from the Purple. The boy was, at least in part, a gift to Laurent. To the Multiverse, Sophie and her love was unique. Her heart was pure and of all humans, all creatures, Sophie alone had a kernel of altruism which extended to greater things. was her friend,

She had not given an afterthought as to her well-being before jumping into the unknown even if Marilyn monitored and orchestrated this nonsense. To the Multiverse, the girl had no survival instinct. Selfless, utterly. Her love for her father was complete, and frightening in its intensity. She felt drawn to enter his mind, but what she really felt was the Multiverse calling her away from her own reality.

She closed her eyes, and with the help of Marilyn, she was once again at the mercy of greater things.

The faint gravity of Mars disappeared. In her heart there was some distant sadness; who was she kidding? Sooner or later, her disabled father would leave her, and his suffering would end. She was fine with that. She felt selfish. How dare she force her father to live in this illusion of a body? Then she felt weak and drowsy. She had lost her mother and her unborn brother. She would rather die than to be an orphan. Luckily, in this immaterial form, she was unable to tear up. Laurent would one day die, but not like this, and not today. She felt the emotions were pouring in from somewhere. She was in partial communion with something holding pain, desperation and revenge.

Sophie had slid the circle of electronics around her head, and instantly lost contact with the strange Electoral Center. This was a bit like traveling to her dream version of Wonderland. She lost all sense of her own body. There was darkness and nothing that reminded her of Laurent's little home.

Virtual reality was to Sophie nothing more than a long and

elaborate man-made illusion. She didn't care about the technical mambo-jumbo. Part of her hoped her father was waiting, in his rocking chair on the porch of his big white house where she had last seen him. He loved the large southern house. But Sophie had a nagging feeling things would not be that easy, something needed her.

The place in which she now floated was strange; this wasn't her father's normal interface. Her head also felt heavier than normal; there was no pain, but she was definitely under some type of strain. She was in a fog, like what she had felt as she was absorbed by LO's music back in the catapult. She had to focus, her mind had to be sharp. She tried to think of the present, her body, and the tube around her. Slowly she began to feel better, more awake. The darkness remained, unrelenting.

***

She was formless, in the dark, and then gravity returned. Her formless body began to fall, drawn forward something and gently accelerating. She'd become a cosmic skydiver, punching through dark layers of invisible clouds. The feeling felt good against her immaterial skin. At first she saw nothing, heard nothing. She just felt the waves hit her face in a rapid succession.

"Daddy!" she shouted in vain.

There was no sound. She was on her way to someplace dark, deep. The feeling of being dragged through invisible walls intensified. She was wasting precious time. In her mind she tried to visualize her father, go to him, and that effort appeared to slow down her progression to the deep pits of this hell. Then, as if she had arrived at her destination, the ballet of cloud layers stopped. This must have been where Laurent was lost. There was a kaleidoscope of colors before she began to distinguish shapes. Slowly the movements, the wind and the colors stabilized.

As her eyes adjusted to the darkness, she began to distinguish shapes. Sophie was floating immobile in a strange new world. The girl began to distinguish rocks and crystals. Everything here was some shade of brown. This definitely wasn't where she wanted to go. She now floated, bodiless in an endless underwater cavern. This place was huge and around were millions of crystal-like structure anchored to the rocks. This felt like being in a deep geyser, with surrounding walls covered by giant snowflakes. Somehow she could see in this muddy soup.

"Daddy!" she tried. There was no up or down. "How could anything live here?" she wondered to herself. This must have been some strange dream created by her father. "Daddy?" she ventured, unsure of herself. This time the words seemed to have an impact on the world around her. As she said it, a shock wave spread in the water, in every direction away from her body. As the sound waves hit the distant walls of the cavern, they damaged some crystals and bounced back like a sonar. This place was weird. No one could dream up something this strange. Somehow, the brown reminded her of the Purple space where she met the rock creature.

"Daddy, where are you?" she tried again but this time without shouting. The weaker voice had almost the same effect on this fragile world. A new wave spread outwardly, snapped of more of the wall crystals and rebounded back her way. She had to be careful.

Then, contrasting with the ambient numbness, she saw in the distance one little dot, a bubble shape made of the crystals of incredible complexity. Inside it, there was beautiful shining lights. She knew this thing was alive. The creature was swimming in the murky liquid. Broken, floating shards, and coming directly her way, evading the light. As it got closer, she could distinguish more of the details inside of it. It was round and looked like a perfect snowball made of a giant snowflake of transparent crystal. This was the most beautiful thing she had ever seen in her life. She had no doubt, this thing was alive. It looked like a jellyfish without tentacles. The bubble came closer and stopped within touching distance.

~ Welcome, visitor, ~ resonated a deep voice. As it spoke, the light pulsed to the sound. This creature was talking to her.

THE ATTRACTOR

"Where is my father?" she asked as softly as she could, not wanting to hurt the creature. There was no sound wave this time.

~ I are sorry. I do not know the creature you call "father." You are the first outsider to enter our world. We do not hold him. He is not here. ~

"He must be here, we're in his mind now. This is his dream."

~ I wish you were right, young one. When you came here, you moved between worlds, realms, facets of the Multiverse; characterize them how you may. I was able to attract you here. I must help you. ~

"You are mistaken. I entered my father's head using a machine. We are in his mind. Let me go. I must find him." Her last word was stronger, it created a wave. The energy hit the creature's outer shell and pushed it back. Sophie saw the few broken crystals on its shell regenerate. It swam back from where it stood.

~ Apologies. I want to help. I understand how confusing this must be for you. I must be blamed; I made you come here. I have a proposition. ~

"Forreal?" said Sophie, dipping her verbal toes into the lake of 2072's slang of the young.

~ This is our world. Many call it the Lower. You are our guest. We mean you no harm. ~

"Let me go. Now."

~ Please, listen to my proposal. It may be useful for you. ~

"I don't care. My father is in danger. Let me go, I have to find him."

~ I apologize. You are, and have been, free to go. Just will it. ~

Sophie needed to find her father. She needed to be next to him and had no time to waste with the bubble creature. She closed her mind's eye and focused hard on her overarching desire to be with him. It worked, and immediately this world called the Lower began to fade. The flooded brown cavern was replaced by darkness. Soon, she could feel a sensation of punching upward through invisible dark walls, she was going back home.

She was leaving this place.

The creature had not lied; it let her go.

She wondered if her impulsive nature was not getting in her own way. She may have been hasty in dismissing the help. She knew the beautiful creature meant her no harm and was in no position to turn down help. Strange things were going on, to say the least. Sophie decided that she wanted to go back to hear the proposition. So she imagined the brown cavern, and the strange little bubble of light. The rising sensation slowed and she felt like she then began to reverse course. She was returning to the place called the Lower. Within moments, she was back where she had been, in the large cavern. The brown color reappeared. The small crystal bubble was still there.

~ I am honored that you have returned. I wish to help. ~

"Why? You must want something."

~ Correct. Yes. I want, above all else, to travel between worlds, and you alone can take me. To do so, I must help you and advise you. ~

"You said you have a proposal. Let's hear it."

~ The line you must walk is thin. There is a task that you need to complete. Something very important. I cannot interfere with your task, but I can help. Others will try to hinder you. I have vast knowledge, collected with great cost and effort over many millennia. I can provide information about these others and other potential pitfalls that may lead to your downfall. Information may be the key to success. ~

"I don't get it?"

He could sense the girl's building frustration. ~ Strange things must have begun happening around you. The law of impermeability, what let you travel here, does not bind you. When you travel between worlds, to search for your father and meet your destiny, I would desire to follow you and help you find him. If you simply will for me to follow you, I believe I will be able to. I vow to remain with you until your task is done, or I die. ~

"Why do you want to leave? Are you a prisoner of this place?"

~ In my world, we do not grow old and die. I am old. Very old. In fact, since I am the oldest known creature of the Multiverse, many simply call me "the Oldest." Since we cannot move between the realms that compose the Multiverse, I've come to feel like a prisoner. Quite frankly, I am bored. I want to see other places, even if for a moment. My survival is inconsequential. ~

"This place is boring in colors. You will love other places." The creature began to pulse with light. Obviously, it was happy. "You will have no body if you follow me, how is this possible."

– Things will work out. Trust yourself. Greater forces are at play around you. –

"What is your name again?"

~ I have many names. Here, I am called the Oldest. ~

She thought briefly. "No. I will call you Liam." Sophie saw a beautiful ballet of lights tingle in the bubble as she named it. She looked up. In the distance other bubbles were approaching.

"Others?"

~ Yes, they envy me. They will interfere. Let us go, please. ~

"Now?"

~ Please. ~

Sophie was not in mood to debate with others. Plus, she found herself liking the wordy little glowing ball. It was cute, in an alien sort of way. It reminded her in a strange way of the rock creature from the Purple but in a much more refined version.

As she did moments before, she closed her mind's eye and imagined she was back with her father. This time, she imagined Liam was there with her, zipping to and throughout the enveloping blackness. She began her way up, smashing through the layers of the Multiverse.

CHAPTER XXVIII

Sophie had a strange feeling. As she soared upward in the darkness, she became aware she was no longer alone. Someone other than her father was holding her hand. Liam was with her. She felt his warming life-force. The creature was acting like a child. She knew he was ecstatic.

~ Amazing, ~ said the voice of her companion. It came from within. ~ This is amazing. May I call you Chosen, or Mistress? ~

"I'm Sophie, just Sophie. We're equals."

~ In my world, we prefer titles. ~

Sophie was exceptional at always getting her way. She even knew she could be a little bratty from time-to-time. She was not, however, going to walk around letting a tiny, glowing, ancient alien calling her "Mistress." "My mother chose this name for me. She passed years ago. It's all I have left from her."

The comment cut Liam like a knife. He had insulted the Attractor with his very first question. ~ I apologize. I will call you Sophie. ~

They continued punching through veils, making their way to a new destination. "What's happening?" asked the girl.

~ I believe we are moving through worlds; you may be perceiving them as if they are curtains, ~ replied Liam.

THE ATTRACTOR

"Worlds?"

~ Yes. Or realms. The terms have become interchangeable. Sadly, we are not in your father's mind. The universe is made of many layered worlds; that is why we call it the Multiverse. The position of these worlds relative to one another is very complex. You alone can move through these worlds. No one, and no technology can allow anything except communication to move between realms. ~

"So why can I? Why me at all?"

~ Sophie, I apologize in advance, but some questions I will not be able to answer. Certain knowledge, especially if shared before you're ready to hear it, might guide you down the wrong path. I cannot answer those questions yet. I do not want to manipulate your decisions. ~

Obviously, her new passenger knew very little about Sophie. She had not gotten to where she was by accepting "no" for an answer. No one, aside from her father, could deny any her requests once she was riled. She'd agreed to ferry him about the cosmos only a short time ago in exchange for information. Now he was refusing to provide it? "Liam, I like you, but you will not keep secrets from me. Do you know the answers to my questions?"

~ In a manner of speaking. ~

"While you are with me, you will not withhold information from me. I won't hesitate to drop you where you stand if you ever do so again. This isn't for you to decide. Things will happen my way, at my pace. You will give me all assistance possible, or leave me. I have no patience for the grownup way of hiding things and keeping secrets."

~ I fear that arming you with the wrong knowledge, gained at the wrong time, could create great harm. ~

"Back on your world, you promised me information. You promised to help me. You also told me to trust myself more. You need to learn to trust me. Your Multiverse seems to have picked me because I'm something that isn't ordinary, and my ways work. Look at what I did with you. I was gone. You'd be in that awful

THE ATTRACTOR

brown cave right this second, and for the next however long, if I hadn't done what I did. I came back to grab you."

The girl was truly amazing. She was correct. Who was he to hold back? ~ I understand, ~ said the creature softly. ~ I promise never to hold any information back. We must speak, then. As soon as possible. ~

Sophie realized she'd possibly been a bit rough with Liam, but she liked her new companion and figured it was best to set things straight from the start. She relented, every so slightly. "At a minimum, explain to me why I cannot know."

~ You are wise, Sophie. ~ Liam had to educate the Attractor. He'd spoken of the fine line she would have to walk, but in truth, his own perch was nearly as precarious. This lore was secret. Divulging it to an outsider was nigh unthinkable, and punishable by death back in the Lower. Yet still, she was the Attractor. Liam fervently hoped he was never going back to his world. ~ First, we must slow down and not enter the next world before you have listened to me. ~

Sophie willed their halt, and their surge of upward momentum ceased. The pair was now standing in the dark, floating in the silence. There were hues, as if the curtains were not opaque.

~ This is wonderful, ~ said Liam. ~ I apologize for trying to hide information from you. ~

"Stop apologizing all the time. Geez, I'm a kid. Everyone always to walk all over me at least once. Don't feel bad."

~ You are the child, how so? ~ asked the oldest creature in all the universe.

"I am twelve. Back in your world, you'd probably just call me 'young one' or something."

~ To me, everyone is young. I do not know how you count in your world, the span of your race's lifetime, nor how your development takes place. ~ Sophie was taken aback by the honesty of the answer.

"Well, it's hard to explain."

THE ATTRACTOR

~ Do not worry. For now it is more important that you understand what I tell you rather than the opposite, ~ said the creature. ~ View the Multiverse as a living creature. A very large creature in which each dimension, each world is a different part of a single body. Each world serves a purpose. We do not understand the purpose of any individual world, but we know there always is one. The Multiverse and its true purpose remain largely a mystery. Each world is important to the whole, and like any living creature, there is a balance between worlds. The Multiverse grows and changes. As part of this aging process, we believe some worlds are asked to disappear. ~

~ Very rarely, the ignorance or the arrogance of the inhabitants of a world results in damage to the fabric of the Multiverse itself. Worlds often fight against extinction, but the Multiverse is extremely resistant. It nearly always finds a way to avert truly severe damage to itself. In exceptional cases, the Multiverse deploys a powerful counterbalancing force to neutralize the existing threat, preventing the destruction of worlds meant to survive or destroy those meant to go. We call this force an "Attraction." It is the Multiverse's last line of defense against an unquantifiable outcome. ~

"Strange word," Sophie mused. "Attraction? Marilyn used that word." Unlikely, Liam thought. He alone knew of the Attraction theory. The creature made a mental note. He had to find out who was this creature called Marilyn. It was inconceivable that this same creature knew his most advanced and guarded secrets and had stolen The Dot.

~ Indeed. We know little about what is intolerable and hurts the Multiverse. Our guesses are always wrong. To understand the way the Universe fixes itself, imagine a long string. Undesirable events bend the string. The Multiverse twists, bends and becomes tangled in unplanned ways. Eventually, the string ties itself into a hopeless knot. Unless repaired, part of the string must be cut away forever to save the whole. ~

Liam, in his brown ball form began slowly floating back and forth in front of Sophie, a symphony of color that bloomed into geometric shapes. It reminded her of nothing so much as those old

THE ATTRACTOR

videos of University Professors lecturing their classes. ~ At the bending point, the heart of the knot, an Attractor appears. We think that the Universe somehow infuses part of itself into an Attractor, widening the Attractor's capacity to store and conduct energy. Then, the Universe fills that new-made void with the most efficient means it can find of igniting the Attractor's potential. ~ Liam ceased his pacing motion and faced Sophie directly. His next words had a new timbre to them; he was no longer lecturing.

"I don't understand."

~ I am sorry. I have no good examples or analogies that might help. I know nothing of your world or its physics to help explain at the moment. I think your world is unique in many aspects. It may actually be based on physical objects. Since our race began, long ago, we have seen five Attractions. The Multiverse has begun its buildup toward the sixth. You are the Sixth Attractor, Sophie. ~

"What does that have to do with me? I'm just a kid trying to take care of her sick Dad! I don't even understand most of what you're trying to tell me!"

~ You are the Attractor. Your mastery of movement across worlds confirms this fact. That being so, I am afraid there is no avoiding your role in things to come. ~

"I don't think so."

~ I understand your discomfort with being told you are different. ~

"It's the second time today."

~ What do you mean? ~

"Back home, a computer told me my brain emits different types of waves. She called them Rho waves. She says they're rare in others. I produce more of them. Like you, she says I am unique and what I do is impossible."

~ I must speak with this computer. I am unfamiliar with these waves. ~ Liam tried to ease her worries. ~ Everyone, in every world, is unique in one way or another. All living creatures have a purpose. Few ever find, before their death, the nature of this

THE ATTRACTOR

purpose. ~

"Things are simple for me, okay? I have to help my father. That's all I care about. Right now he needs me."

~ Then we will try to go to him, help him. ~

"I tried that already, and I wound up meeting you in the brown world."

~ I am mostly to blame for that. I drew you to me. Your powers exist to serve a higher purpose. The road you must take will lead you to where you must go. I am happy to see the Multiverse agrees with my theory. In the eyes of the Multiverse, I am going to help you achieve your purpose. This brings me great satisfaction. The theory of Cause and Consequence is true. ~

"How come you speak English? That makes no sense."

~ You are observant little one. Apologies, I meant Sophie. ~ She liked Liam. His voice was very respectful and reassuring. ~ The worlds and realms of the Multiverse are extremely different from one another. The laws of physics in each are different: even your bare glimpse of the Lower has made that obvious to you, I am sure. The uniqueness of these laws is the reason why realms do not fuse into a single unified place. The barriers between each are strong. All worlds rely on some type of energy, but few use waves, and fewer yet use cold, hard matter. I think your world is unique in that it relies almost exclusively on matter. If you are, as I suspect, from the world we call the Cold, the arrival of your world will be a treat to most.

~ As you can imagine, life in each world is completely different. All creatures differ, and a physical barrier exists between worlds. Nothing can pass except some very limited volume of information at key points, precious portals. But each time we communicate, somehow language is never a barrier. ~

"Are you talking about something called the Dot?"

Liam was stunned. ~ You know of the Dot? ~

"Yes. I don't know what it is, but Marilyn used me to grab it. I heard her mention it. I think it's true." The implications to Liam of what Sophie said were severe. Somewhere, a creature from the Cold had used the power of the Attractor to steal the Dot. This feat required a level of technology and understanding of the Multiverse that he had not thought possible. Liam silently redoubled his determination to investigate this creature. Depending on her motivations, this "computer," whatever that was, could be a very great threat to all of existence.

~ Most interesting, Sophie. I have many questions to ponder, especially now. My most important role is to continue to inform you on the workings of the Multiverse. Let me continue. It is of vital importance that you understand the process that lets you move and communicate between worlds. You need not understand every nuance of the science, but the foundational why of the thing is important. Understanding this next lesson will help you understand why the Multiverse helped you reach me, and will reveal to you where we are going next. I hope, for your sake, to your father. ~ Liam gleamed softly in what Sophie had taken to indicate a small smile.

~ Imagine knowledge itself is a physical thing. It would have a series of layers inside of a structure, yes? The top layer is formed with information you just collected, like knowing me. Below is a layer formed by who you are: your memories. You grabbed Marilyn's name from this layer. Still further below resides the instinctual layer. The primitive layer. This one helps control your body, and it is a bit of a mystery. In each realm, the third layer, like the realm it springs from, differs from all the others. Between the instinctual layer and the layer of self, some possess to regulate retention, speech, communication and know what is important and what is not. It cleans things up. ~

"Are you always this complicated?"

~ Apologies. ~

"Stop apologizing. Is that layer what we call dreaming?"

~ Interesting. ~ The girl, while appearing not to care about his information actually was paying attention. ~ Yes. It is common for species to rest, but not all of them dream. In any event, by making a simple bridge of communication between the lower and deeper layers between individuals, two people can bypass language and communicate easily. I am sure as the Attractor, you can travel and move freely in the Multiverse, you can adapt to the laws in each world, and you can communicate on such a deep level. What you saw, was built for you. ~

"I don't really think I need to know this. Please, my father is sick."

~ I must not interfere, Sophie. Do as you please. Don't let my words distract you from your path. ~

"Don't worry about that part. I see you don't know me at all, yet."

In a fraction of a second, they resumed moving between worlds. The feeling of passing through curtains began anew. They were now going in a different direction; she felt it.

~ This is incredible. ~

"Really?"

~ Dear one, millions of years, thousands of worlds, the Multiverse picks one, you. This gift and curse is beyond explanation. Revel at this beauty as I am sure such demands will have a price. ~

Slowly, they reached their destination and finally stopped moving. All around Sophie was a diffuse purple color. It was less solid than smoke, and not exactly light. She had seen this place before.

"Do you know where this is?" asked Sophie.

It took Liam some time to adapt. He was visibly happy, his inner flashes of light hued purplish by the space around them. ~ The space, it is ~

"Big?"

~ No, it is colored. Is that Purple? ~

"I guess if you never left your world, you would know only the color brown. How sad."

THE ATTRACTOR

~ I am fulfilled. Others spoke of color, we could only imagine the concept. ~

"Wait until you see my world, this is boring to me."

~ We call this world the Purple. It is a world that touches yours. You may be interested in knowing that its inhabitants are hostile, aside from one boy named Malik and they have recently declared war on your world. ~ The pair was floating in this quantum world. In the distance was a deeper purple patch where the creatures lived. There were no rifts around.

"How can you be old and not have been here?" asked Sophie.

~ Only you can travel between worlds. Others rely on recreated images. At the moment, though, your mind empowers most of my functions. I'm being expanded, by proxy, through your own link to the Multiverse. This world is amazing. I can die happy now. This world has very little materiality; most of this place is made of waves. It will be difficult for you to understand this place. As I said, the creatures here are hostile. ~

"Can you do me a favor, can you avoid talking about dying, okay?"

~ What? ~

"You said you could die now. As a child, I have already seen my share of people who die. I don't like death. Stick around, okay?"

Liam was touched by the request. For her, he had to remain strong. He was her guide and teacher, ancient beyond words and as alien as the girl could imagine, but somehow he was overwhelmed by the situation. He was old, so old. For billions of years, the only thing which had kept him alive was his determination to get a glimpse of another world. In minutes, he had gone from being locked in the Deep and having to understand what had happened to the Nexus to talking to the Attractor herself. She was kind, mature, and intelligent. He was in the Purple, actually in the Purple, with the Attractor! His life had found its purpose. Now she was asking him to remain. He would see her home, to the Cold.

~ Yes. I apologize, my wish is to help you, Sophie. In my

world, we have no children. We do not procreate. In exchange, we are immortal. I feel a very strong empathic bond to you, Sophie. Is this normal? ~

"Everyone feels that way toward me. I got used to it. At first I figured it was pity for my dad's condition, but now I think it's different, those Rho waves."

~ Your father, is he all right? ~

"No. He was attacked."

~ Can I help? ~

"Maybe. I needed to enter his mind. He's lost his normal human senses, so I'm forced to visit him using a computer interface. Whatever attacked him seems to have made that impossible. I wonder why I'm back here again? Why me? What's the thing about the Attraction? Why would the Universe care about me? It's ridiculous."

~ We should speak more of the Attraction. Each time in our past, when we entered an Attraction, a single creature was given great power to fix things to the benefit of the Multiverse. ~

"Power?"

~ Yes. Attractors are very powerful, but not in terms of energy. I believe they are causes to consequence duality. ~

"You lost me again."

~ These are complex matters, Sophie, few truly understand them. Our theories are also only that: theories. ~

"What does that have to do with me?"

~ You have the power to do impossible things. Your power will grow as the attraction nears its apex. You will be able to act outside of logic, probability and science. I think that nothing you can conceive of, can will, is outside of your reach. In most worlds, stories are written of gods, you, sweet one will be given the powers of a god. ~

"Like saving my father?"

~ Correct, but with one limitation. The Multiverse's needs supersede yours. You cannot change something it does not want changed. ~

"The Universe wants my father to be sick?"

~ I wish I had all the answers. Since the Multiverse is large, we would imagine that the Attractors are equally large, energetic things, but they are precisely the opposite. Always small and vulnerable individuals. You are the Attraction. It is in the Cold; your unique world. What you need to do, and how you need to do it, is a complete mystery to you and I. You were chosen, not I. I fear that by telling you about the past Attractors, or by giving you my opinion, you may be misled into acting like I would. That would defeat the purpose. The past Attractions failed, at least in part, for that reason. They listened to others. ~

"Funny."

~ What? ~

"You don't know me. Everyone says I am stubborn and only do things my way. If the Multiverse wanted someone who could ignore others and their opinions, however good, that's me for sure."

~ I am happy to hear this. You truly are a gift. ~

"Don't start pampering me, Liam. I don't need that. Everyone is always nice to me. I need you to say the truth, always."

~ Why did you pick the name "Liam" for me? ~

"It's personal."

~ I'm sorry if I have pried. ~

Sophie felt like her newfound companion deserved more respect. She owed him an answer. "Liam is the name I wanted for my baby brother. My parents picked William."

~ You have a brother? ~

"He died before he was born."

~ I am so sorry. ~

"I don't know why I picked that name for you, maybe I

shouldn't. But I like it."

~ I am truly honored. The Multiverse has extremely complex ways of expressing matters. What I know is that something in your world is twisting and hurting the Multiverse at its core. Whatever it is cannot be stopped by normal forces of reason. This thing is so important that unless it ends or changes, large parts of the Multiverse will end. Your task, I believe, is to correct this problem. You must use this power in a way that you alone can. ~

Sophie was not really concerned by the story. She cared little about the world, life, or even herself. Her only real concern was her dad. He was alive. Could he be the thing hurting the Multiverse? Doubtful. He was easy to stop, he was only one badly hurt, barely alive man.

"Electoral," she said.

~ What? ~

"Forget it for now." She really liked Liam. What she just said could wait.

~ You said you have been here before? ~

"Yes, in a dream. What do you know of this place?"

~ The inhabitants are extremely hostile. A race called the Metils. They are to us extremely large creatures. From what they said, they are very small by your world's standards. The Metils live in hot zones, a patch of deeper purple. ~ He looked around and saw the patch. ~ There, that must be one of their cities. They are highly structured creatures. They love technology and war. They now claim that rifts between your world and this place are destroying them. They referred to a boy named Malik who claimed to have traveled between worlds. Were you there each time he did so? ~

"Is my father here?"

~ I do not know. It is doubtful, since this is not your world. Only the Attractor can shift worlds. ~

The light purple space around them began to change, warp, as if light was being diverted by a series of large mirrors. Invisible prisms were moving in all directions. Sophie felt like she was in a house of mirrors with moving walls. She began to hear explosions and all manner of noises, but she did not feel any different. By the look of things, they were standing in the middle of some type of battlefield being oblivious to the detonations around them.

"What is going on?"

~ As in my world, you, or rather we, appear to be incorporeal. We are beyond their reach. We are ghosts, observers if you wish. Obviously, they see us and are trying to destroy us. This situation is, once again, a technical impossibility. What a wonderful observational opportunity. ~ He seemed completely unperturbed that aliens were trying to kill them.

The ballet of explosions went on for several minutes. Soon, the creatures in the distance made of spinning rocks realized they were wasting their time and ended the attack. Instants later, a new type of weapon was used with the same lack of results.

~ Sophie, thank you so much. ~ Liam was at the moment the happiest creature in the Universe. For an old person, he sure was acting like a kid, thought Sophie. The Metils began their approach floating in this strange color sky. They reminded her of the firefly. As they came closer, she was able to distinguish their inner structures. These were little balls of rotating and spinning rocks, like complex clouds of dust gravitating as little planets with orbiting moons. Sophie had just seen two life-forms from two different worlds within minutes, not to mention her voyage to the Electoral Center and her eye-to-eye introduction to Marilyn. She was handling this situation very calmly, with her usual detachment.

"Stop!" ordered the approaching creature. The voice was decidedly rude.

"I'm not moving," she snapped back, with equal rudeness.

"Stay there!" barked a second Metil.

"I hate bullies," said the girl to the second creature.

She was neither scared nor intimidated, just calm but forceful. She decided to move to the side by a couple of feet just to show the creatures she could. With her mind, she willed it and they moved. Liam was impressed by the girl's reaction.

THE ATTRACTOR

"I said don't move." As the creature talked, lights of multiple colors shone between two layers of orbiting rocks. Sophie moved again. The same creature spoke again, but this time with a softer tone. "Who are you?"

"Sophie. My turn to ask a question. Where is my father?" There was a silence.

"We have no one here like you."

"Why am I here?"

"We do not know."

"Someone is holding me here?" Sophie spoke out loud to Liam.

Liam replied. ~ No one here has the power to hold or summon you. We are here because this is your path. You must see or do something in the Purple before we can depart. ~

"Who spoke?" the Metil asked, nervously. He'd heard Liam's voice but was unable to see his body. Sophie was tired of wasting time. She wanted to leave. She tried to concentrate on the image of her father, but this time nothing happened. Then she remembered Electoral's test. She focused on the white plush dog. She waited a moment, then opened her eyes. She was still facing the little floating rock creature.

"Liam, are you still here?"

~ Yes, why? ~ "Nothing."

"We know of the creature from the Cold named Sophie," said the Metil. "How?"

"Is Sophie your name?" it ventured. "Yes."

"You injured Malik, one of us. He told us you followed him here and you talked to him. We have images."

"The firefly? I injured no one. Where is he?"

"He left to meet you. We believe he is in your world."

"Why am I here?" asked Sophie once more.

"We do not know," replied the Metil.

"Not you. I was asking my friend Liam." She now was calling Liam a friend.

"Who is this? Who are you talking to?" asked the Metil.

"A friend, from a place…"

~ "Don't!" ~ Liam tried to interrupt.

"…. a place he calls the Lower."

Words exchanged quickly between the creatures. They knew of the Lower, of course. Moments after the Oldest had threatened this entire world with destruction, a creature from his world was physically present with the creature from the Cold named Sophie. Since their weapons did not work, they started to retreat.

"Wait!" said Sophie.

The creatures were no longer communicating. They were pulling out, moving as fast as they could away from them.

Sophie already liked Liam her new travel companion..

CHAPTER XXIX

The Electoral Center

The interview of the father of Electoral aka Marilyn resumed in the beautiful Martian backdrop. "Don't you just love Marilyn? Not a boring day at the office." Georges was trying to reassure the journalist on their way back to the interview room. "The thing back there with the kid, the numbers, that was awesome, no? Measuring this shift was something humans could have done for a long time. It took my creation to do it. She thinks humans are unique in the universe, we alone have these waves; remind me why we should fear her. She reveres us." Milly smiled and waited until the official interview to resume.

Georges walked up and sat back in his large seat. The view of the Martian landscape somehow seemed different, more realistic as the thin atmosphere in the sky turned to a deep green. Electoral's explanation had made the universe seem alive.

"As the journalist, I should try and play devil's advocate to incite more emotion from you, but I won't. I concede. In the back there was both entertaining and educating television. Surely thousands back home are already working hard to decipher what all that really means. Let's continue with a mature interview if you want," she resumed, "why mars, why go through the trouble of running this game from millions of miles away. This sound counter-productive?"

Georges' glass of Mountain Dew was empty, so he grabbed Milly's. "Can I?"

"Of course." She answered. He drank from her cup and put it back empty. On the Martian horizon, behind them, Marilyn was now broadcasting the most majestic sunrise.

"For lack of a better term, we were kicked out."

"Excuse me?"

"The boot. One day in 2061, while we were back home on Earth, a terrorist tried to detonate a 300-kiloton nuclear bomb in downtown Paris. This remains a guarded secret. Marilyn stopped him. Minutes later the man was arrested. The incident itself didn't scare the Generals, but they freaked out about Marilyn's capacity to stop the detonation fearing they had also lost their power to destroy mankind. They came to us without as much as a thanks for saving millions. They were very worried about our capacity to interfere with their own weapons of war. They wanted assurances their toys still worked.

"Marilyn was blunt. She explained she was not about to let some idiot destroy the entire human race or the environment. That included Generals, governments, or god-almighty. She explained that non-military civilians were now off-limits. An attack against powerless people would be considered an act of war and she would step in.

"As you can imagine, the bullies and thugs forming these groups took issue with losing their power. Every bad guy united against us. They also found support with other groups that specialized in mass domination and control. During the final of Electoral 2062, while she was running the final simulation, these thugs united and attacked at her weakest, during the game. They launched a digital offensive, multiple software programs and even physically blew up servers. They even used virus technology."

"I don't recall any problem during the final."

"Precisely. They tried. They failed miserably. There was a

perceptible microsecond delay in the feed if you watched closely, nothing more. Go back and see; the character of Marilyn was getting out of a caravan, she looked up, and there was a small noise in the sky."

"So they were upset."

"You bet. Marilyn took away their toys. Better yet, they realized they were playing with empty guns. The next day began a political push to get her offline. Unable to destroy her, they now wanted Electoral turned off. They could make the game illegal. Marilyn insists this game truly elects the one person capable of doing what she says she can't and the survival of mankind might depend on this game."

"Marilyn truly believes the game must continue at all costs?"

"Yes. The preservation of the game was part of our compromise to leave. We agreed to exile ourselves to Mars in exchange for the Electoral 2072 competition. She cares because of the Feed."

There was a long silence as the journalist looked down at some notes she wrote in the palm of her hand. "You talked about the Feed, it's important?"

"Yes." He would say no more.

"What's next for Georges?"

"What do you mean?"

"You, Georges, in ten years? Twenty? Where do you plan to be? What do you want to do?"

"Ten years ago, if you asked me the same question, I would never have guessed I would be here in this strange fortress of solitude, like Superman at the North Pole." Georges knew his basics. "She has plans, great plans, I know that. I don't know what they are anymore. Her intelligence is such that I no longer understand what she really thinks. What I do know with my heart? She is working hard for the good of mankind. She truly loves us and admires us."

"How can you tell?"

"I guess I'm not really objective. I know her. I have spent the last forty years with her. I know in my heart. I begged her to stop Electoral; to let some other software run it. I wanted to walk out on her. She simply said, 'Nothing is more important to our world's survival.' She now believes Emilio has a gift which can save humanity, nothing less.'"

There was a long silence.

Milly turned to look at the image of Marilyn floating in the sky.

"What did you mean by that?" she asked the artificial intelligence directly.

The image of Marilyn answered, "When a child has a tough day in school, arriving home, she can feel overwhelmed by it all. A parent can't explain the importance of education to the child. I can't explain the importance of the Electoral process without endangering its positive role on your race. But believe me, this game is more than it looks. Much more. Simply put, the game warps the deterministic events surrounding the survival of your race. Borrowing the famous Schrödinger analogy of his cat in a box, the game makes sure that when the box is finally opened, the cat will be alive. I want your race to survive the next challenge and sadly I fear things are moving temporarily faster than I would like."

"Are you saying that Emilio's role in the current events is not what it seems to us?" "Very perceptive Milly. Precisely. All I know is that as of today, if the game stops, I fear the days of your race are numbered. If the game continues, your race stands a chance to see the next step."

"How?"

"I can't say more. I beg, one day you will thank me for my silence."

Milly understood what Georges meant. She felt so small. The universe was vast, alive, and human science truly was in its infancy. The game and President Emilio had a role to play in what was going on.

THE ATTRACTOR

***

In the Berlin diner where President Emilio was becoming nervous by the turn of events, he couldn't help but smile. This was the best validation of his intuition. His plans were important and relevant. He turned to his lieutenant Patrick and simply said, "We have work to do."

CHAPTER XXX

The Purple Dimension

"Liam, are you still there?" spoke young girl floating in the light Purple world.

~ Sorry to have shocked them away. We have a reputation in the Lower, they are truly annoying ~ he tried to explain, ~ I did declare war on them a short time ago for daring to attack your world. Happy to see they took me seriously. ~

"You defended us?"

- Yes, but in full honesty, I would have done the same had they attacked any other world.

"They looked petrified."

~ They should be, ~ said the elder, proud of himself. ~ I threatened them with mass destruction unless they changed course. The Metils sadly follow only one course, the most violent path. Too many races remain close to that instinctual layer we talked about earlier. I fear your world may be in danger. ~

"No need to be judgmental." Sophie looked around. In the vastness of this purple space, millions of little spinning objects were appearing like bubbles. She had not seen this the last time she entered this place with the creature in her dream. She looked the blooming rocks. These were growing debris like mushrooms or popcorn coming in existence from nothing.

"Liam, what do you think those are? A weapon?" Sophie loved having an invisible companion.

The little floating structures looked to like pieces of strawberry granola hitting each other in some type of exploding popcorn motion. Each floating rock was different yet similar like a kaleidoscope of colors. Some of these could be living structures.

~ See how these things grow, I believe our own size is unstable. These structures are not really growing; I fear we are shrinking. The Purple is a pure wave worlds, it has no real matter. Everything you see is not really there. -

"What about those?" she pointed.

- You are the Attractor, if these worlds, my world did not have some physical reality, you would be unable to understand and view them. I believe your own mind and the Multiverse is constructing these things to help you travel. ~

"This is crazy."

- Cute one, we communicate, I speak your language and even just used the word 'cute' which is a foreign concept in my reality. The powers the Multiverse is giving you are beyond imagination.-

"What can we do?"

~ The weapon is forcing us to shrink out of the world. We appear to be shrinking fast. Try to imagine yourself as if you are growing, getting larger. See yourself back at the size you were at the time of our arrival. You can also look at a piece of rock and image it getting smaller. ~

Sophie had no eyes, but in her mind of this ghost form, she imagined what Liam had just suggested. With some effort, one rock stopped growing and stabilized at the size of a mountain, then it began slowly to shrink in size. Liam was right; they were shrinking. Slowly, with concentration, the scaling stopped. As if someone had hit a rewind button, the debris began to shrink back down into smoke. The purple color of the world returned.

~ We are back! How wonderful! Truly exceptional. ~

THE ATTRACTOR

She opened her mental eyes. "Where are we?"

~ It seems we are back where we arrived. Look to the left, in the distance. Notice the difference in color in this area. We spoke of how the darker purple zones must be their cities. The creatures live from warm areas where energy seeps in from the stars from your own world. We must find the one linked with your Sun. ~

"This darker spot is the location of our Sun? You just said this world was smaller than ours."

~ You are a quick learner. That is correct. Distances, like sizes, vary in every world, often strangely. The only thing constant is the direction of time. In every layer of the Multiverse, time unfolds in one direction: forward. It does, however, unfold at varying speeds in different places. ~

Sophie was intrigued by the concept of an alien city. "Sun creatures, I like it. Why are you upset at them?"

~ The inhabitants of this particular place have broken several rules of the code of conduct that exists between worlds. We, from the Lower, are the enforcers of these rules. ~

"Your race is powerful. Do you know what we look like to them?"

~ Good question. I have no idea. ~

"You told me no one can walk between worlds. Why would they expect to see you here?"

~ You are right, those were my words. No one can directly come here. These are not the brightest creatures. Generally, my race conducts retribution indirectly between worlds. We can always increase or decrease the energy pouring into this place. Energy seeps naturally between worlds in many different ways; energy always originates in one place and goes to another. What we can do is regulate these flows. We generally abhor doing so, because it forces the Multiverse out of equilibrium. We cannot know the purpose of the Multiverse. ~

~ The Metils are primitive in many ways. They do not understand the rule of impermeability, nor any of the Multiverse's other laws You already have a deeper knowledge of worlds than most here. They found and opened a communication door, and as the rules require, we had to connect it to the Nexus. They must think our arrival here is somehow linked with the coming war. I am puzzled by their vast understanding of your world. ~

"Well, isn't my arrival linked with the war?"

~ Again, young one, you shame me with your wisdom. ~

"Liam! Don't take this the wrong way, but all this world stuff is getting way too complicated. If I learned one thing since the accident that took my family, it's this: don't sweat the details. I just want to save my father, be with him, and give him joy before he leaves me. If I was picked, it's because I'm easy to predict. Or maybe Electoral is playing games here. Maybe you're only part of the computer reality. All this could be of her doing. I'd never know the difference."

~ I cannot give you the reassurances you seek. If our interaction is made up, this would be a rather sadistic game to play on one such as you. ~

Sophie was on a long road, far from where she really needed to be. She had been lost before, when the courts first ruled against her and refused to give her custody of her father. She then went to Mars, then to the stupid Center, and now she was lost here, in a different world. She just had to be herself, keep calm, and think.

"I think I know how to get out."

~ You do? ~

"Yes. If this was really a world, a different place, we would not be simply ghosts. This means we are part of my dream. My body is home. I assume we are both in my mind, I am stuck in my own dream, unable to enter my father's mind."

~ I am not one to disagree. You are the Attractor. I am here to help. ~

The strange couple began to move in the direction of the city. She just needed to find Malik, and at the same time she would find her father. At least that was the plan.

THE ATTRACTOR

Their flight through the Purple resumed.

~ Sophie, how old are you? ~

"Twelve." The number proved rather useless without additional data. He did not want to burden her.

~ How do you measure your age? ~

"These are years, we have seasons. Four seasons in a year. Why?"

~ We need to find the age of this Malik creature. it is possible you both were born at the same moment. The Multiverse loves these types of non-coincidences. Was there any important event in your world on the moment of your birth? ~

"None that I can recall. Boring day, November 21. Why?"

~ The Multiverse stacks alignments. Each time it does anything, timing is always very fortuitous. The last four Attractions were driven by dates. Maybe I am seeing too much in this. ~

"Well, the last five did not work, you said. Maybe the date thing was not really that important. I'm more of a spur-of-the-moment girl. I like to flow with things. But this year my birthday will be special."

~ How so? ~

"The finale of the Electoral 2072 simulation, run by Marilyn. It will be on that day."

~ The creature which used you to grab the Dot? ~

"Yes. Is that important?"

~ Most definitely. ~

"How so?"

~ That, I do not know. ~

***

THE ATTRACTOR

Then the colors around her began to fade. The world disappeared slowly. Sophie opened her eyes and saw the doctor's face.

"She's back!" The doctor exclaimed.

"Finally!"

She was in a thick bed and not in the tube. "Why am I here?"

The voice of Marilyn Monroe replied from a distance over the Doctor's shoulder, "Did you think about Oscar, the white dog?"

"Yes, a while ago."

"I saw a peak, a signal. I apologize. I pulled you out immediately, you probably were in a place with a different time unfolding."

Sophie waking up slowly. She was alone in a nice girl bedroom with the doctor, the others were absent.

"Did you see anything, did you find him?"

"I saw something different. How long was I gone?"

The doctor looked around, wondering if she could say the truth. Finally she replied, "A little under a week. We all were nervous."

Then there was a voice in Sophie's head.

~ Amazing! ~ said Liam in her mind. Susie did not hear it. Sophie smiled. Liam, her friend, was still with her.

Sophie stood up, on screens she should see the face of the computer goddess, "Marilyn, did you just hear another voice?"

"No," she answered.

~ Perfect, ~ said Liam in her mind. ~ Is this the creature who store the Dot? ~

Sophie stayed silent but in her mind answered, "yes."

Marilyn Monroe obviously could read her internal voice from her eye movements.

She stiffened. Liam's voice in her head simply added, ~ Oh my, this will not be simple. ~.

Here ends book 2: The Multiverse
The story continues in book 3: Electoral 2072

ABOUT THE AUTHOR

Alain Villeneuve is a Canadian Aerospace & Nuclear Engineer, a U.S. Patent Attorney, a British Solicitor and an International Law teacher. His passion for Sci-Fi authors and famous physicists forced him to author this series in honor of the great classics. After a decade in Europe, he now lives in Seattle Washington with his husband Kai, and his two terriers. He dabbles in endurance sports, archology, sociology and finance.

Made in the USA
Monee, IL
31 August 2022

c1fe2d1e-d9ef-48e8-b3f8-935074e256c0R01